A Not So Misfit Odyssey

Written by J.F. McCarney

"... Gather Round..."

"A mystical journey awaits you on the following pages. And when you encounter words from distant lands—like Dehesa (day-HAY-sah), where our story begins—a quick look in the glossary at the back will reveal their meanings. Each chapter also holds an Acorn of Wisdom, a special nugget of knowledge to help you understand our world better."

"¡Vamos! (Let's go!)"

Illustrations and original artwork for A Not So Misfit Odyssey were done by Kyrie Foutz

For the friends who touch our hearts...

Table of Contents

Prologue:
A World in Change

Acorn of wisdom:

An acorn takes fifty years to grow into a mighty oak tree, but only a day to cut it down.

Before there were smartphones and selfies, and before cities grew bigger and bigger, the world was a colorful tapestry of wild places. In *Spain*, for instance, ancient forests called *Dehesas* stretched as far as the eye could see. Their mighty oak trees were passed down—first from great-grandfathers and great-grandmothers, then to grandfathers and grandmothers, to fathers and mothers, and finally to daughters and sons. These oaks dropped golden brown acorns that fed everything from tiny mice to massive Iberian pigs. As solar panels glistened in the distance, one of those oversized Iberian pigs foraged, cracking a golden acorn between his back teeth.

… His name was… Juanito…

Unbeknownst to Juanito, far across the ocean, in a place called the *Amazon*, trees grew so tall they seemed to touch the stars. Their branches were so thick with leaves and vegetation that they provided a thick green roof that sheltered millions of creatures. During the rainy season, rivers wider than twenty football fields flowed through the jungle, carrying life-giving water to both animals and the people who had lived there for generations.

... But the world was changing everywhere...

Back in Spain, some of the ancient oak trees began to sicken. Their once-strong branches drooped, and fewer acorns fell each year. The farmers who had tended these trees for centuries worried—not just for themselves, but for all the creatures who called the Dehesa home.

In *South America*, the sound of chainsaws echoed through the jungle. Where trees once stood, vast farms appeared. Farmers who had tilled the land for generations were forced to leave... many of them moving north, leaving behind the only homes they had ever known. Animals like jaguars, monkeys, tropical birds, and all sorts of exotic creatures were forced to wander, searching for new places to live.

Some said this was the price of progress… Others wondered if there might be a better way… a way where people and nature could thrive together…

… This is a story about seeking that better way…

But mostly, it's a story about a pig named Juanito who learned that the greatest journeys are not about where you are going…

… but who you are traveling with…

Chapter 1:

The Golden Dehesa

Acorn of Wisdom:

An oak tree on a Dehesa can provide food and shelter for about two hundred species of animals and up to one hundred different kinds of plants, making it one of the most life-supporting trees in the world.

One early morning, as the sun peeked through the clouds and a few modern wind turbines spun lazily on the distant hills, Juanito, a huge Iberian pig, roamed the fertile Spanish Dehesa. His dark, shiny form towered over the other pigs as he devoured the scattered acorns beneath the old oak trees.

Even the *toros bravos*, those fierce bulls bred for the arena, gave Juanito a wide berth as he pushed his way through the oaks. The air was thick with the earthy smell of acorns and the melody of magpie birds that chirped in the branches of the trees.

Juanito admired himself as he saw his reflection in a water trough. *Who is the most handsome pig in all of Spain? You are Juanito, you are,* he thought. A nearby piglet rolled their eyes as Juanito continued to admire himself.

The other animals, unconcerned, continued with their happy grazing. But Juanito could not shake a strange feeling that something was not quite right. He raised his snout in each direction, but it was not a smell he was concerned about…

… the furrow in his brow confirmed it was more of a feeling.

"Juanito! Juanito!" a squeaky voice cut through the silence. Juanito turned to see a small rabbit racing toward him. It was Conejo, his long-eared friend.

"Did you see they took Paco this morning?" Conejo exclaimed.

Juanito scanned the hillside. *Now that Conejo mentioned it, the Dehesa does seem emptier somehow.* Juanito sniffed the air again, and this time, he caught a whiff of something that made his bristles stand on end. He glanced around the Dehesa and nodded to Conejo.

“As a matter of fact, it appears more than half of my swine friends have not joined us today,” Juanito agreed.

Conejo's whiskers twitched as he jumped up onto Juanito's back. He leaned over to whisper in his friend's ear.

“The word is that a mysterious disease is killing the oak trees,” Conejo murmured. Juanito gave a quick look up at what once was a mighty oak. He nodded in agreement with his fluffy tailed friend’s words.

“Uhm, I think you are right, Conejo. There are fewer acorns on the ground,” Juanito nodded.

Juanito used his large girth to push away other pigs so he could hoard more of the tasty, nutty gems. He knocked away a group of younger pigs with his rear-end as he swept all the choicest nuts into his own private pile. Two frustrated miniature pigs nearby started fighting over a single acorn, their squeals echoing across the once-peaceful meadow.

“Juanito, don't you think you should share some of those? The little ones have barely eaten today.” Conejo watched the younger pigs huddle together in the distance.

Juanito snorted, sweeping more acorns into his pile with his large snout. "Why should I? I am the biggest and strongest… that's just how things work. The mighty oak drops its acorns, and I take what I want. It's the natural order, my floppy-eared friend."

Conejo jumped down off Juanito's back, his ears twitching with concern. "So, the natural order means you take all that you wish, while others go hungry? When you ate so many acorns last week and got sick, I didn't leave you to suffer alone. I stayed up all night with you."

"And I appreciate that," Juanito replied, though he didn't stop gathering. "That's why you're my best friend. You understand me." Conejo stepped in front of Juanito, blocking his path to a rather large acorn.

"Do I?" Conejo sighed. "Sometimes I wonder if you understand yourself, Juanito. We should all help each other out, not just think of ourselves."

Juanito paused briefly, looking at several piglets desperately foraging for acorns. For a moment, something like guilt flickered in his eyes. But then he spotted another cache of acorns and waddled toward them, leaving the hungry younger pigs behind.

“They'll find their own food,” he called back to Conejo with a snort. “They just have to look a little harder…”

Conejo sighed and just shook his head…

Suddenly without warning... The roar of engines disturbed the calm silence.

Big trucks with large animal pens in the back thundered over the hill. With a surprised silence, Juanito and Conejo observed a group of men, who appeared to be *vaqueros*, skilled Spanish cowboys, who jumped out of the trucks and gathered the remaining toros bravos.

The bulls roared in confusion and anger as the vaqueros lassoed them, using prods and shouts to herd them onto the trucks. As they were led away, the earth seemed to shake with each step of the massive beasts.

As the dust settled and the trucks rumbled into the distance, a heavy silence fell over the Dehesa. The remaining pigs huddled together, their oinks soft and uncertain. Juanito, ever the optimist (if a bit self-centered), cleared his throat.

"Maybe the bulls were causing the trees to get sick. So, they being taken away will mean more acorns for us, right?"

The pigs all oinked, eager to believe in any explanation that might restore their sense of security.

CRACK! One of the diseased oaks gave way, its mighty trunk splintering as it toppled to the ground. Juanito and Conejo managed to leap clear as the ancient tree crashed down just inches from where they stood.

"Uh, I don't think the bulls caused that," Conejo deduced.

Panic spread through the young pigs like a dark cloud…

But Juanito stood still, staring at the fallen oak. For the first time in his life, he felt afraid. The Dehesa, his paradise, was changing… and not for the better. As he gazed over the rolling hills, Juanito realized their world would never be the same.

"Conejo, I think we might be in trouble."

The rabbit nodded, his ears drooping. "What are we going to do, Juanito?"

"I don't know, Conejo." Juanito's eyes twitched at the uncertainty. He turned his mammoth frame around in a circle, looking for anything that might make him feel better; but there was nothing near or far that put him at ease.

As the two friends stood side by side, gazing out at their changing world, the wind picked up and whispered through the leaves of the remaining oaks, carrying with it the promise of adventure… and the hint of danger ahead.

In the following days, the scramble for acorns became a daily battle. Conejo would guide the piglets to freshly fallen nuggets, to the frustration of Juanito.

"You are lucky I don't eat grass, Conejo. If I did, I would be just as inconsiderate of your favorite food as you are of mine," Juanito complained.

This went on for another week or so. The oaks became noticeably more dry. Very few acorns fell to the ground. The Dehesa continued to wither. The once-lush paradise became a shadow of itself, with more trees succumbing to the mysterious disease each day. The remaining pigs, including Juanito, fought over the scarce acorns.

One gloomy morning, the silence was shattered by the arrival of several vehicles. Two sleek cars led the procession, followed by a convoy of large trucks with animal transport containers. Juanito and Conejo watched from behind a withered oak as a group of humans emerged.

"This does not bode well," Conejo blurted out. Juanito eyed the men and tried to dismiss Conejo's doubts.

"Don't be so sure, Conejo. Maybe they are here to fix the trees," Juanito said.

A tall, slender man wearing a pricey suit emerged from the lead car, concern visible on his face. This was Don Alfonso, the owner of the Dehesa. Beside him stood Señor García, the farm manager, an overweight man with a thick mustache and a bright red face. Juanito and Conejo listened to every word.

"I'm sorry, Don Alfonso," Señor García said, his voice heavy with defeat. "We've done everything we can. But with the oak tree disease destroying our acorn crop; we are left with one choice: sell the remaining pigs."

Don Alfonso nodded as he scanned the barren landscape and then turned toward the wind turbines and solar panels on the far-away hillside. "We can only do so much to embrace mother nature. But this drought is beyond our control. Who would have thought a simple tree disease could destroy generations of work in mere months?"

As the two men talked, a third figure emerged from the second car. This was Don Lorenzo Valdez, an Argentine businessperson known for his flamboyant tastes and extravagant parties. He was a thin, short man with slicked-back hair and an expensive watch that sparkled in the morning sunlight.

"Don Alfonso!" Don Lorenzo called out, his voice booming across the quiet hillside. "I hope you don't mind me dropping by. I have traveled a great distance."

Juanito's ears perked up at the new voice. He turned to Conejo and whispered, "Who's that?" Conejo's nose twitched. "I don't know, but he doesn't smell like he's from around here."

Don Lorenzo circled Señor García, eyeing him like a predator. "So, these are the famous Iberian pigs, eh? The ones that make the ham that cost more than gold?"

García nodded. "Yes, señor. The absolute best. Each one raised on a diet of the finest acorns. Or... they were, before all this." Garcia eyed Lorenzo up and down with a return gaze.

"Your reputation precedes you, Don Lorenzo. Some people say the logging activities of your businesses in the Amazon contributed to the drought that caused this disease to our trees."

Don Lorenzo seemed amused. "Please, no need to be so formal with me, Señor García; just call me Lorenzo." He leaned into Señor García who seemed uncomfortable that Lorenzo was so close to his face.

"So, you think what I do on the other side of the world affects this hillside?" he chuckled. He eyed Don Alfonso, Señor García and the hillside.

"Absurd!" he laughed aloud. "Enough of such nonsense!"

Lorenzo's eyes sparkled with interest. "I was told you have the finest Iberian pigs on the peninsula. That is why I came here today!" Lorenzo eyed all the pigs.

"And what will become of them now?" Lorenzo asked.

Don Alfonso sighed. "They'll be processed into ham, though most should be feeding on acorns for much longer."

Juanito felt his blood run cold. He turned to Conejo, panic rising in his voice. "Did you hear that? They are going to turn me into ham already!"

"Uh, you know that was your fate anyway, right?" Conejo said.

"Yes, of course, but not so soon. I still have many moons and sunsets to admire," Juanito lamented.

A gate on an empty metal animal pen on the back of a truck slammed open.

Conejo's eyes were wide with fear for his *porcine* friend. "You have to get out of here, Juanito! You must run!"

But Lorenzo's voice rang out again before they could move as he spied Juanito. "Wait a moment! What about that one there?" He pointed at Juanito, who froze in terror.

García followed Lorenzo's gaze. "Ah, you mean Juanito? He is our prized pig. The biggest one we've ever raised."

Lorenzo's face split into a wide grin. "He's perfect! Listen, Don Alfonso and Señor Garcia, I have a proposition for you. The Festival of Hams is coming up in Buenos Aires."

Don Alfonso and Garcia both frowned, caught off guard by the comment.

Lorenzo's mind was going a mile a minute. “I knew I'd find such a beast here. I just knew it.”

Don Alfonso and Garcia were perplexed at his outright giddiness.

“Why are you so excited at such a troubling turn of events for us?” Don Alfonso protested.

“My father used to say: One man's misfortune is another man's opportunity,” Lorenzo uttered.

“So, you revel in our losses?” Don Alfonso fired back. Lorenzo paid him no mind.

He made his way over toward Juanito. He eyed him like he was a long-lost treasure.

“What if I were to buy this magnificent beast and display him at the Festival of Hams in Buenos Aires? They will see I can accomplish more than my father--” Lorenzo cut himself off.

He regained his composure. “And after the festival... well, he'd make quite the trophy ham, wouldn't he? I dare say the largest ever seen at our festival!” Lorenzo gleamed.

Don Alfonso hesitated, switching his gaze from Lorenzo to Juanito. “I don't know, Señor Valdez. It seems cruel to ship him all that way just to--”

“Nonsense! I will pay you double... no triple! I want this *prized ham-to-be...*”

Juanito and Conejo stared at each other. Their eyes became misty, understanding the reality of the situation at hand... Juanito nudged Conejo with an affectionate lowering of his snout. He then proceeded to dig in his hooves and stared at Lorenzo and the approaching farm hands. He was not going to leave his dear Conejo…

But Juanito, no matter how massive his size, and how determined he was to not leave Conejo, was no match for the will of the humans… At least today he wasn’t.

With a nod from Don Alfonso, the farm hands moved in. Juanito tried to run, but months of comfortable living had left him slow and out of shape. Within moments, he was corralled and guided toward one of the waiting trucks.

“Goodbye, my friend,” Juanito whispered.

Conejo hopped back and forth but knew there was nothing he could do.

“Don't forget me!” Conejo whispered back.

Conejo watched with concern as his friend was taken away. The rabbit's small form shook with sobs as the trucks rumbled off, carrying Juanito and the other pigs to their fate.

Lorenzo climbed back into his car with a satisfied smirk on his face. “See you in Buenos Aires, my most *prized ham-to-be*,” he chuckled as the car zoomed off.

Conejo found himself alone on the deserted hillside. The once-bustling Dehesa was silent, save for the mournful whisper of the wind through the sick oak trees.

“I won't forget you, Juanito,” Conejo whispered as he watched the convoy of vehicles leave. He eyed the empty fields where he once had so much fun with Juanito. He turned and watched the trucks become smaller in the distance. Conejo slowly made his way over toward his burrow where his siblings waited.

“Is it true they took Juanito away?” one of his brothers asked.

Conejo just sadly nodded his head... And so, Conejo hopped away with his siblings, together, away from the Dehesa to find a new place to call home.

The fading odor of acorns gave way to the guttural screeches of a couple of vultures that landed on a decaying oak tree branch.

In his cage on the back of the truck, Juanito took one last look at his beloved Dehesa as it disappeared behind the dust kicked up by the truck. He pressed his snout up against an opening in the cage. “Conejo, my friend,” he whispered, though he knew his rabbit companion was far beyond earshot. “We both know the truth, don't we? This... this is goodbye forever.”

… Juanito smiled through his moist eyes and drifted back to the first day he met Conejo. He was one of twelve kits born that day. The other eleven newly born rabbits always stayed close to their mother. But Conejo was adventurous. He was attracted to Juanito and even tried to eat acorns with him... which made Juanito laugh. “Silly rabbit, eat the grass and the berries," he would tell him. They played together day after day, a mismatched pair to anyone who watched them... But to each other they were the best of friends... inseparable... until today...

… No, after today... they would not be together any longer...

And so, Juanito let out a deep sigh. He squinted at his cherished Dehesa, now nothing more than a speck in the distance, knowing he would never return again…

Chapter 2:
A New Continent and a New Friend

Acorn of wisdom:

Argentina's name comes from the Latin word for silver because early explorers believed the country was full of silver mountains.

After an uneventful sea journey of many days, a weary Juanito wobbled onto the deck of a large cargo ship. Behind him a crew member with an electric prod poked him to move him forward. Juanito grimaced every time he was poked with it.

Juanito froze, coming down the gangplank leaving the rusty cargo ship. His eyes widened in a mixture of fear and awe as he caught his first glimpse of…

... The massive city that stood before him: Buenos Aires, Argentina. The bustling sounds and unfamiliar smells washed over Juanito with a wave of uncertainty.

From black and yellow-colored taxi cabs honking at each other, to the sound of a traffic cop blowing a whistle that no one listened to... the chaos of Buenos Aires was nothing like his treasured Dehesa. On either side of the main streets stood magnificent, classic, European style buildings. Each one was made from soft gray, limestone granite that made Argentina so different from many South American countries.

A street vendor on a large three-wheel tricycle made his way through the cavernous streets in between the towering buildings, selling local savory *chorizo* sandwiches. "*Choripan*! Get your choripan!"

Lorenzo and one of his workers greeted Juanito at the bottom of the gangplank. The worker, a shy young man named Santiago, in his early twenties at most. He wore traditional peasant wear of a long-sleeved, faded cotton shirt and matching pants... a hole in his worn boot let his toe say hello to Juanito as he looked down at Santiago's shoes. His wide straw hat had seen better days for sure.

The one noticeable thing that seemed a bit out of place was Santiago's large name tag badge he wore above his tattered shirt pocket…

… the gold 'LVE' logo of Lorenzo Valdez Enterprises was imprinted on it in bold cursive letters above his name.

Santiago and Juanito eyed each other. Juanito noticed there was a certain sadness in Santiago's eyes. Juanito had no way of knowing that Santiago had been separated from his home too. He lost his small farm that was left to him by his parents who both passed from the poison of pesticide spraying by nearby mega-farms. His land was deemed useless and confiscated. His former home was taken over by the powerful mega-farm and Santiago had nowhere else to go except to the big city. But he felt out of place just as much as Juanito did.

"Well, don't just stand there! The Festival of Hams has begun! Lead him to the square!" Lorenzo chastised Santiago.

Lorenzo was a spectacle all by himself. Dock workers and others snickered behind his back at his attire. He was dressed in what looked like ceremonial traditional

Argentinian cowboy gaucho wear; a very odd outfit for someone who had never worked with animals in their life.

On his head, an expensive, brown leather cowboy style hat, with a pure silver inlay that sparkled in the sun. His fancy cowboy clothes included a white embroidered shirt monogrammed with the letters 'L.V.' for Lorenzo Valdez and very fancy boots.

Two elderly men playing chess at a café table in a nearby park, looked up from their game. "Ah, there goes Lorenzo Valdez, pretending to be a gaucho cowboy again," one muttered. "Just like his father."

"The difference is… unlike his father… Lorenzo, is all show, no substance," his companion replied.

"Remember when he was twelve at his first ham festival? Poor kid couldn't even look anyone in the eye after what happened."

"How could I forget?" The first man chuckled, shaking his head. "His father, Don Emilio, paraded that prize pig of his around like royalty, only for it to knock Lorenzo into the mud right in front of half his classmates who I think are still laughing."

The second man studied the chess board, then eyed Lorenzo and shook his head. “Do you remember what his father said to him that day?”

“Sure do... ‘you continue to be nothing but an embarrassment to me, Lorenzo.’”

The first man hesitated, his expression darkening. “And then there was his mother...” He let the words hang in the air, his tone heavy with unspoken sorrow.

The second man frowned, adjusting his bishop chess piece as if to shift the conversation. “Checkmate,” he said.

Lorenzo walked in the street with Santiago and Juanito in tow, his smile and posture as proud as could be. The people stared at him as if he were a side show in a local circus.

Juanito could not take his eyes off of the festivities. His head turned side to side taking it all in. From booths that sold *churros*, those sweet, sugary, cinnamon delights, to a strange, dark booth with a velvet-draped table, Juanito was mesmerized by it all. Behind the table sat an older fortune teller lady in a flowing skirt and a colorful shawl. She shuffled a large deck of *tarot cards* and finally picked one out… It was one with a dreary moon image… the classic fear card… the one that represented the unknown… possible danger? She eyed Juanito and shook her head in disappointment as she showed him the card.

Juanito just put his head down and quickened his pace…

Several farmers holding their prized hams were standing on a stage. A man, wearing a white butcher's coat holding a blue ribbon walked past the different farmers and ranchers... He walked ever so slowly, whispering to two other judges who walked next to him. But all eyes were focused on the man in the white butcher’s coat…

Finally, he stopped in front of one of the farmers who held his ham out in front of him... the farmer looked up with such hopeful eyes. Would he be rewarded as others had been rewarded at this most prestigious ham festival?

The man in the white butcher’s coat pinned the ribbon on his ham. The farmer jumped for joy. Everyone cheered and applauded as the other farmers and ranchers left the stage, dejected.

Juanito watched all the farmers as they all eyed him in return. Their frowns let Juanito know his presence in any future ham festival would not be appreciated.

And then all eyes turned to Lorenzo as he made his way forward. A forlorn Santiago was right behind him reluctantly leading Juanito to the center of the square by a thick rope around his neck. Lorenzo gestured to a band and on queue they began to play a combination of *Cumbia* and *Tango* music. He even had *Tangueras*, women dancers, in traditional, elegant, colorful costumes behind him.

Lorenzo, jealous of the attention for the winner, gestured with both hands to his band to play louder.

Gasps of awe rippled through the crowd, followed by excited chatter and the lifting of countless cell phone cameras as a bewildered Juanito made his way forward.

"Ladies and gentlemen!" Lorenzo Valdez's voice boomed through a megaphone. "Behold the eighth wonder of the world: the largest pig ever to grace this festival!"

Juanito sighed, frustrated with being the center of attention.

A nondescript voice rose above the crowd.

"Trying to step out of your father's shadow, are ya?" an anonymous spectator yelled out.

The comment made Lorenzo stop for a second. Angry, he tried to find who made the comment in the crowd. But he could not. What he did notice was a young boy huddled with his father in a doorway, hands pleading for spare change...

Lorenzo paused; were his eyes a bit moist? He reached into his pocket and tossed a handful of coins to the pair. As the father hugged his son close in gratitude, Lorenzo's face flickered with an emotion Juanito could not place and a puzzling response.

"At least your father stayed by your side," Lorenzo muttered. Then, as quickly as it had appeared, the moment vanished, replaced by Lorenzo's usual show-off attitude as he continued.

"*¡Dios mío*! He is enormous!" a woman exclaimed.

"I've never seen anything like it," a man in a chef's hat marveled. "Imagine the feast we could have with him right now!" Juanito trembled and eyed the chef...

Lorenzo's eyes flashed at the comment. "Ah, but my good sir, <u>that</u> would be a waste of potential! This incredible creature will be the star of a future festival when he has cured properly. I promise you; he will become the most exquisite, expensive ham the world has ever seen!"

As the festival ended, Juanito was transported to a holding pen at a nearby slaughterhouse owned by Don Lorenzo. Alone and depressed, Juanito huddled in the corner. Cold concrete pressed against his side. Distant city sounds filtered through the walls. A rat scurried past. It eyed him curiously and vanished into a crack.

The smell of damp hay and metal filled his nostrils, so different from the earthy scents of home. Santiago reluctantly put a metal grommet holding a tag-like item in Juanito's ear.

"Sorry, my friend. It is just protocol," Santiago explained. He then filled a feed trough with slop and left the pen.

Juanito sighed and whispered to himself. "Not exactly the tasty acorns from the Dehesa that I am used to…"

"Baaa... quite the showstopper, aren't you, big guy?"

Juanito was startled by the voice. He looked up to see a sheep that was so woolly that it was almost spherical.

"Barev, im ungér!" the wooly sheep exclaimed.

"Uh, okay Ungér is it? I am Juanito."

"No... Juanito... I was saying hello. 'ungér' is just the sound for the word 'friend' in Armenian," the sheep said, her accent unlike any Juanito had heard.

"Well, nice to meet you, Ungér," Juanito introduced himself.

Frustrated, the sheep just shook her head. *"Che!* No!*"* she uttered... "ungér" is just the sound of the word we would use for your word "friend." ... or as they say back in *Yerevan: ընկեր."*

"Uh, I really don't understand. So, should I just call you friend?"

"Ayo! I mean, yes... just call me 'Ungér' if that is easier for you."

Ungér studied the enormous Juanito.

"Where are you from, Juanito?" Ungér asked.

"I'm an Iberian pig... or I was."

Ungér waddled closer. Juanito blocked Ungér from the animal slop that Santiago had put in a trough in front of him. Ungér seemed confused, but didn't address Juanito's selfish behavior...

“Iberian? That is in Spain. I have heard it is beautiful there,” Ungér stated.

Juanito nodded. “It was. The rolling hills of the Dehesa, the ancient oak trees, the acorns,” he sighed. “But it's all changing now. What about you? Armenia? Is that a long way from Argentina?”

Ungér's eyes took on a faraway look. “Ah, Armenia. Land of mountains and ancient stories. My ancestors fled during the dark times; when those with hate in their hearts tried to eliminate Armenia,” she paused. “Some of us have been wandering ever since, searching for a place to call home.”

“That sounds terrible,” Juanito murmured. “Don't you have a flock here?”

Ungér seemed evasive. “I uh, got separated from my flock in the port. One minute, I was with them, the next, well, here I am now. Waiting to be sheared and then mutton stew, I am sure.” Ungér’s voice trailed off.

“At least they're keeping you alive for now,” Juanito offered. “My demise is near. They will soon cure my hindquarters in salt so they can be the star of a future ham festival.”

Ungér tilted her head. "Ham festival? Is that a big deal in Spain?"

"Oh, you have no idea," Juanito said. "*Jamón ibérico* is the pride of Spain! It is not just food; it is an art form. The best hams are cured for two years or more and cost hundreds of euros per kilo."

"Wow," Ungér bleated. "That does sound special. But have you ever tried Armenian string cheese? It is called *chechil* and it's so stretchy you can braid it!"

Their conversation continued, each trying to outdo the other with tales of their homelands' cultural wonders.

"... and each year the humans run with the bulls in the streets of *Pamplona.* A few of those horned beasts make a 'point' about their distaste for captivity if you know what I mean," Juanito winked...

"Did you know we Armenians made the first wines?" Ungér proudly proclaimed.

"I don't know about that, us pigs have been whining forever," countered Juanito.

Ungér could not contain her bleating laughter.

“Not <u>whine</u>, silly... *wine.*” If Ungér could roll over with her laughter she would.

“That is what I said,” a confused Juanito came back.

“Oh, Juanito, you know so little about this world, don’t you?” Ungér chuckled.

A friendship grew… very quickly. Maybe it was nerves or maybe it was that they were forced to be together. For whatever reason, it was clear they made the most of being there at that very moment.

As night fell and the temperature dropped, Ungér huddled alone in her corner.

Juanito did not want to be forward but moved close to Ungér, blocking a cool breeze that came into their pen from the dreary hallway.

“You know,” she said softly, “we Armenians, we have a saying: 'A shared burden is a lighter burden.' Even wolves hunt in packs, and sheep stay in flocks. No one survives alone.”

Juanito shifted uncomfortably. “Well, I've always managed fine on my own.”

"Have you?" Ungér asked, her gentle voice carrying no judgment. "Is that why you're here, in this pen, destined to be someone's *prized ham-to-be* before your time?"

The words caught Juanito off-guard. As the night wore on, they shared more stories.

"… and once Conejo warned me of squirrels stealing my acorn stash… you should have seen them run as I oinked at them as loud as I could!" Juanito laughed.

Ungér was truly amused and laughed every bit as hard as Juanito did. Ungér stopped laughing and just stared at Juanito. Something about him made her nod her head over and over.

"What? What is it?" Juanito asked.

Ungér moved closer to Juanito. She then said the strangest thing.

"I enjoy you, Juanito…" They shared mutual grins.

Juanito was taking a liking to this sheep.

"You know, Juanito, all I want is to find another flock and start a family. For an Armenian sheep like me, family is everything. It's how we've survived for generations, kept our culture alive."

Juanito nuzzled her. "That sounds wonderful, Ungér. I hope you find that someday." The silence between them reminded them there was little chance of that...

"And you, my friend?" Ungér asked. "What do you hope for?"

Juanito was quiet for a moment. "I... I do not know anymore. I have lost so much. My home, my best friend, Conejo. But meeting you, Ungér, reminds me that even in the darkest places, we can find light and friendship."

As they drifted off to sleep, Juanito realized that though he had lost his old life, he had found something new and precious here. He was grateful for this moment of connection in a world that had seemed so cold and lonely.

Over the next couple of days, Juanito and Ungér did what good friends do…

… They shared more stories...

... "But my favorite was the holidays. Everyone was so happy; some of the children tried to feed me *Gata*, a sweet bread," Ungér smiled as she reminisced. And as if to make a point to Juanito... "And I would share it with my flock."

"I'm not too good at sharing," Juanito stated the obvious.

They watched with heavy hearts as their fellow animals were led away and never returned. Juanito always kept an eye on their pen's door, wondering when he would meet his culinary preparation and his demise. The few moments of laughter with Ungér were replaced with… despair.

One morning, as Juanito and Ungér huddled together, Santiago and another worker approached their pen, their voices clear and loud in the quiet slaughterhouse.

When the workers set down fresh vegetable scraps, Juanito smiled, and surprised himself, and Ungér, by nudging some toward her. The unselfish act caught Ungér by surprise.

The first worker froze in place as it was his first time seeing Juanito. "Man, look at the size of that Iberian pig! Don Lorenzo wants him to meet his fate at the salter tomorrow; begin curing as a prized ham." Juanito trembled as he understood what the words meant.

"I think that is such a waste," Santiago protested. He then crouched down, his face level with Juanito and Ungér, and spoke softer, as if sharing a secret with the animals.

"You know, I heard there's a place that's even better than the famous Dehesa. A magical place where animals like you could be free and happy."

Juanito's ears perked up, and he nudged Ungér to listen.

Santiago enjoyed that his coworker listened to him for a change. He took center stage as if standing on an imaginary soap box.

Santiago lowered his voice, his eyes taking on a distant look. "Last year Don Lorenzo sent me on a cattle drive on the *Pampas.* Over a bottle of *Caña* liquor one night, an American cowboy told me of a place up north called The River of Nueces. A paradise where animals roam free among endless oak and pecan trees."

"Another one of your fantasies?" his co-worker scoffed. "Where is this magical place?"

Santiago crouched down to Juanito and Ungér's level. "In a place called *Texas*. They say the acorns there are bigger and sweeter than any in Spain. The humans there are too busy with their cattle to bother the other animals," he sighed wistfully. "Wouldn't it be wonderful if such a place existed? Where creatures could live in peace?"

Juanito was wide eyed like a child on Christmas morning. The first worker rolled his eyes.

"Maybe it only exists in that bottle of Caña that American cowboy and you drank," Santiago's co-worker countered. "You're nuts, Santiago. You and your misplaced love of animals. Even if such a place exists, we can't all live on acorns and nuts."

Santiago was mesmerized by Juanito and Ungér. He petted them both. He pointed to Juanito to make a point to his co-worker. "Oh yeah, look at him. He eats only acorns and vegetable and grain slop. Look how big and strong he is."

"Alright, alright, Mr. Vegetarian," the first worker chuckled as he cut Santiago off. "You and your imagination. Why do you even work for Don Lorenzo then?"

Santiago's smile faded as he stood up; faced with the reality of his internal compromise. "Working for Don Lorenzo was the only job I could find." Santiago looked around at all the other animals in pens down the hall.

"If it were up to me, I would let them all go. I wish I had somewhere else I could make money." Santiago put out both his hands with palms up. He looked at the left one.

"On one hand, I don't think we should eat animals. We should live in harmony with them..."

Santiago then looked at his open right hand with his palm up.

"But on the other hand, I know many others don't feel that way..."

His co-worker had heard enough...

"You accept the money from Don Lorenzo for working here with both those hands. Now back to work or we will both be out on the street with our hands up begging for money!" he lectured Santiago.

The workers moved away, still debating the merits of their jobs.

Juanito turned to Ungér, his eyes wide with joy! He waddled a three hundred and sixty degree turn in one direction and then reversed and did it in the other direction.

"Careful there Juanito, you weren't built to move like that," Ungér smiled.

"Did you hear that?" he exclaimed. "A place even better than the Dehesa! A place where I will not be turned into ham. A place where I can roam free... forever! We must go there, Ungér. We must escape!"

Ungér was skeptical. "Escape? Juanito, we are in a locked pen in a slaughterhouse. How do you propose we do that?"

Juanito's mind raced. "I... I don't know yet. But we must try! Think about it… you could finally have a home, and I could live in a new Dehesa. It is our only chance!"

As they huddled together, whispering plans and possibilities, fate intervened in the form of Santiago. He came back and started mopping the concrete hallway outside each locked animal pen. Santiago stopped and kept staring at Juanito and Ungér.

Santiago sighed as he petted them both but focused on Juanito. It was obvious in Santiago's eyes he struggled with Juanito's fate-to-be.

Santiago knocked over a bucket of soapy water on purpose in front of their pen gate. Juanito was at first confused, but then his eyes lit up as he smiled at Santiago, who smiled back.

"Ungér," he whispered, "I have an idea. When they come to feed us, we will..."

… The next morning...

Santiago arrived with their food and Juanito put their plan into action.

He charged forward, appearing to rush for the food. Santiago feigned surprise as he slipped on the soapy puddle and fell, leaving the gate wide open.

"Now, Ungér!" Juanito whispered.

"Help! Uh, help. They are free!" Santiago uttered, as he shooed them on their way.

In a flash of determination, Ungér rolled herself into a ball and barreled through the open gate, knocking over two more workers.

Juanito followed close behind, his enormous bulk creating chaos in the narrow corridors of the slaughterhouse. As a worker came close, Juanito butted him away with his enormous right hindquarter and the worker went flying up against a wall. As another tried to grab him, Juanito butted that worker even harder with his left hindquarter with such force, the worker's body smashed up against an exit door. WOOSH! The door flung open!

Ungér smiled back at Juanito as they broke free into the street outside the slaughterhouse.

WEE-OOO! WEE-OOO! Alarms blared as they burst out into the early morning light of Buenos Aires. Santiago stood at the exit door, feigning concern as he helped the dazed workers to their feet but couldn't hide his smile as Juanito and Ungér waddled into the busy streets of Buenos Aires.

The city was just waking up; streets filled with bleary-eyed commuters and morning vendors setting up their stalls.

"Which way?" Ungér bleated. Her eyes were wide with panic and hope.

"North!" Juanito oinked. "Always north!"

Juanito waddled in one direction, then turned to another direction.

"Uh, which way is north?" Juanito wondered aloud.

Ungér eyed the morning sun, smiled at Juanito, and took a few steps north.

"When you wander as much as I have, you learn how to use the sun to know which way you are going," she confidently explained.

"It's this way, Juanito…"

Juanito's hooves clattered on the pavement, and Ungér's woolly form bounced beside him as they thundered down the street.

People jumped out of their way, coffee cups flying, and a fruit cart toppled over, sending oranges rolling in all directions. The fruit cart tumbled down a street hill and cars screeched to a halt! Chaos reigned supreme. One thing led to another. People tripped over each other chasing the fruit. Everyone watched as a large watermelon rolled and tumbled down the street till finally…

SMASH! It splattered on the steps of a large stone courthouse. A flock of pigeons swooped down and feasted on the unexpected morning buffet. Their cooing and flapping wings announced their gratefulness to the oversized pair of Juanito and Ungér for the delicious bounty…

Juanito and Ungér, wide-eyed at the sight, hurried off as best they could and the mismatched pair hid in a quiet park, panting out of breath from their escape.

"I can't believe we did it!" Ungér gasped.

Juanito grinned, excitement still running through him. "Believe it, my friend. This is just the beginning of our adventure."

"You think we can make it?" Ungér inquired with a hint of uncertainty in her tone.

Juanito's expression softened. "I don't know," he admitted. "But I know that we're in this together whatever happens. And somehow, that makes me feel like anything is possible."

As Juanito trudged beside Ungér, he felt the weight of his past with Conejo lightened by the hope of this new friendship. For the first time, the vast unknown ahead seemed less daunting.

But their moment of freedom shattered like glass.

"Find that pig!" Lorenzo's voice thundered from a nearby street where he gathered with a small posse.

"I think they are long gone, Don Lorenzo," Santiago sheepishly uttered.

"Nonsense! I will find him! He will not escape me!" Lorenzo screamed.

Lorenzo got up in Santiago's face. "I can't believe you were so careless! I heard you talked to them of some paradise?"

Santiago eyed his coworker with disdain, who lowered his head.

"But Don Lorenzo, I talked in jest. They are a pig and a sheep, they can't possibly understand what I say," Santiago defended himself.

Upset, Lorenzo pushed Santiago aside.

He then focused on the task at hand: find Juanito at any cost.

"A bonus to the man that finds him!" he yelled. "I must find him!"

Meanwhile on the adjoining street out of sight of Lorenzo, Juanito and Ungér melted into the chaotic maze of Buenos Aires leaving Lorenzo's voice far behind...

Chapter 3:
A New Direction...

Acorn of wisdom:

A single kapok tree can grow over two hundred feet tall, as high as a 20-story building; and its trunk can grow wider than a car is long.

Over the next few days, Juanito and Ungér found themselves far past the city's outskirts, exhausted and lost. They made their way out of Argentina by sneaking up a loading plank on the back of a truck load of chickens. As the truck traveled north, they passed through the *Gran Chaco* region of *Paraguay* and its savannahs.

"The air smells different here," Ungér noted. "Like spices and earth... and freedom." Juanito smiled as they watched the countryside through the flapping tarp of the poultry truck.

"This land at first seems like nothing but a dry forest and then a bunch of thorny shrubs, only to border on a jungle again," Juanito commented.

Ungér peaked out at a giant *armadillo,* those armored back creatures that looked like a giant rodent. A rare black *jaguar* moseyed on its way with two cubs close behind.

"Woah, what are those things?" Juanito wondered. Ungér just watched the different creatures go on their way.

"That hard backed one is called an armadillo… and that large black cat is called a jaguar," Ungér matter-of-factly stated.

Juanito eyed her, in awe of her knowledge. "How do you know all this stuff?" Juanito wondered aloud. Ungér eyed the countryside and especially the jaguar and her cubs.

"Her cubs are born blind at birth. They must stay close to their mother so she can nourish them and keep them safe from predators until they get older," Ungér stated.

Juanito tilted his head, curious. Ungér noted his confusion.

"I know so much because nomadic sheep let us know about other lands... I think we are in a place called Paraguay... or maybe *Bolivia*... but it is the same everywhere it seems," Ungér sighed. She sadly stared out at the countryside.

A small *cassava* farm stood in the shadow of a massive commercial operation, where local *Ayoreo* farmers struggled to harvest their root like crop. Behind barbed wire fences, rows of corn and soybeans stretched endlessly. Dust from passing trucks loaded with the same corn and soybeans from the huge corporate farm, settled over the modest cassava plants.

The poultry truck that Juanito and Ungér rode in stopped to let the corporate trucks pass. Ungér couldn't help but notice a weathered farmer in a nearby tiny cassava farm wiped his brow as he spoke to his son. "Keep that bandana over your mouth, *hijo,*" he coughed.

"Papa, why must we work so hard for so little?" the boy asked.

"It wasn't always that way," the father replied, his eyes fixed on the loaded corporate trucks in the distance. "But it is the way… now."

Ungér was surprised to see a pack of *coati,* long-tailed racoon like creatures playing mischievously in a tall, tough *Quebracho* tree. Off by herself was a mother coati in a secluded nest. She was letting several small kits of her nurse on her multiple teats.

Juanito noticed Ungér's longing look. Seeing the jaguar and her cubs and now this nursing coati, brought a sadness to Ungér's eyes… this was her dream… to nurture offspring of her own.

"I promise you, Ungér, I will help you find a flock… so you can raise a family." The look between them surprised both of them. Juanito was thinking about someone else besides himself.

As they drove along, the truck rattled as *cicadas* buzzed, and a humid mist rose from the Paraguayan jungle. The truck struggled as it traveled toward the high plateaus of the *Altiplano* area in Bolivia. Ungér would casually make a comment of what she had heard about each place. A few animals appeared from time to time staring at their truck as they raced by. Their traveling companions, the chickens, cackling loudly. Ungér would raise her voice so Juanito could hear her.

"… and those are *llamas*… no, *alpacas* I think," Ungér pointed out. A graceful smaller one ran in the distance. "Oh, I know for sure that is a *vicuña,* they like the cold too," Ungér confidently said.

"They all look the same to me," Juanito lamented.

The positive smile on Ungér's face made Juanito realize something.

… Hope is all he had.

He had no idea whether The River of Nueces exists; and he was even less certain he would be able to find it… But right now, they were stuck on this truck with all these chickens, and he was heading north…

… Well, at least he hoped so…

They were fortunate that from time to time they stopped, as boxes of fruits and vegetables and other food items were loaded on and off. Hiding in the corner out of sight, Juanito and Ungér smiled at each other as they pilfered a few food items.

“Try this,” Ungér whispered, nudging a ripe mango toward Juanito. “Mmm,” Juanito mumbled through a mouthful. “Nothing like acorns, but still good.”

Ungér just shook her head at Juanito.

“There's a whole world of flavors beyond acorns, my friend,” Ungér chuckled quietly.

After what seemed like many days, their truck finally stopped at a poultry factory. Morning sunlight flooded the truck as the rear door opened, revealing an endless sea of metal cages. But the humidity of the Paraguay jungle and cackling of the tropical birds made them realize they had to face what was ahead of them…

“I think this is the end of the line,” Ungér whispered. Their chicken companions croaked loudly as workers began unloading nearby trucks. When the workers left the loading plank on their truck unattended, Juanito and Ungér made their escape. They paused only once to look back at their traveling companions, knowing there was nothing they could do to help them.

As they went on their way, the terrain changed so quickly. The signs of deforestation were everywhere. Stumps of large *kapok* trees dotted the now scarred rain forest. Tree branches and brush burned in controlled fires. Chain saws littered the ground near humans who loaded timber on trucks.

But Juanito's main concern seemed to be with some beady eyes he kept noticing in the shadows. The eyes followed behind or above them as they walked through the not so dense rainforest. Juanito could sense something, and his head was on a swivel as they made their way forward.

"I feel like we are being watched, Ungér," Juanito whispered.

Then, a sultry voice rang out from a vast, green kapok tree.

"I knew it, some chatty strangers. A pig and a sheep far from home, are we?" the voice hissed.

Juanito and Ungér froze as a colorful boa constrictor, four meters long, slithered down to meet them, scales shimmering in the moonlight.

"I'm Paulo," the snake said, their voice gentle and welcoming. "And you two look like you could use a friend."

Paulo slithered closer to them.

“You’re lucky. Even in a shrinking jungle, there's always room for those seeking shelter.”

Juanito eyed the snake with caution. “I'm Juanito, and this is Ungér. We're trying to reach The River of Nueces, but we're being pursued by an angry businessman named Lorenzo Valdez.”

Paulo's eyes widened. “Lorenzo Valdez? That monster and his family have been destroying my habitat for years with one of their businesses in the Amazon.”

“What do you mean destroying?” Juanito, asked.

“His logging company is destroying everything… mahogany, cedar, teak. What used to thrive in my ‘living room’ is now a coffee table in some human’s,” the hissing snake complained.

“The local farmers who lived in harmony with the land lost everything to large companies like his and others from the north.” A distant grinding sound from an iron ore mine punctuated Paulo’s words.

"Then where did the farmers, ranchers and other workers go?" Juanito questioned.

"North," is all Paulo said.

Paulo paused. Anger seemed to rise in them. "We're at the *Bolpabra* - where the borders of Bolivia, Paraguay, and *Brazil* meet," Paulo explained.

"Just as much damage has been done here as there is up north deeper in the Amazon," Paulo explained. Paulo eyed some barren jungle, it's emerald, green plants and trees removed with a few chainsaws resting on the ground. Paulo quickly slithered away in disgust.

"So, this is not the Amazon?" Ungér followed up.

Paulo eyed Ungér and Juanito. "The Amazon is vast and spreads over this area too. But the heart of the Amazon is deep in Brazil many kilometers north of here. I fled it hoping I could find a place that wasn't being destroyed… but I must say… that is proving to be more difficult than I thought," Paulo hissed.

"Ever since I was a hatchling, things have been changing for the worse," Paulo uttered.

“Hatchling?” wondered Ungér. “I thought large snakes are born live, not an egg?”

“We are not an egg, but some still refer to us as hatchlings. We slither into this world as a juvenile snake and immediately are on our own. We must find our first meal and leave our mother’s side from the first day we are born. Everywhere I’ve tried to settle and call home has been destroyed,” Paulo hissed loudly.

Dejected, Paulo just eyed the dwindling vegetation around them.

“Come, I know a safe place where we can talk,” Paulo sadly commented.

Paulo led them to a train yard where steel giants gleamed in the moonlight. A distant whistle and clanging box cars warned of human presence.

“Watch your step,” Paulo cautioned. They made their way past scattered tools toward an abandoned boxcar.

“It smells like rust and oil,” Juanito observed, wrinkling his nose.

Unattended loading planks led into different train cars. Paulo led them into the abandoned boxcar and eyed Juanito and Ungér.

"You are out here by yourself?" Ungér asked Paulo.

"We boa constrictors are a solitary kind. Except when we come together to mate," Paulo explained.

Paulo felt an unusual level of comfort being around Ungér and Juanito. Paulo spoke as if they were holding something in for a long time.

"I've always felt unique from most of the other boa constrictors anyway," Paulo stated as they kept a watchful eye out the boxcar door. Ungér tilted her head. "What do you mean?"

Paulo's eyes took on a faraway look. "It's hard to explain. I've always felt different," Paulo said softly, keeping a keen eye on the boxcar door, then turned to Ungér. "Like I never quite fit in my own scales. Imagine if everyone insisted you were a goat when you knew you were a sheep."

Juanito turned his head, curious. "That sounds, uh, confusing."

"It was," Paulo agreed.

"Well, I know I am a sheep; and I know I want to start a family." Ungér chimed in. She smiled at Paulo. "But that's me, Paulo. You be you. It is only right to embrace who you are," Ungér followed up.

"Thank you, Ungér. That means a lot to me." Paulo hissed.

VROOM! VROOM!

Their conversation was interrupted by the distant sound of truck engines.

Juanito was totally confused. It was Lorenzo. "How--?"

"Quick," Paulo said, "into that other boxcar! I know these trains - this one's headed north. It'll take you far from here." Paulo eyed Lorenzo and his cronies in the trucks and then their new friends…

"Oh, heck. I'll help you get wherever you are going," Paulo surprised them.

As Juanito scrambled into the new boxcar, Ungér tripped over a rusted toolbox and fell.

"Hurry, get up, Ungér, hurry!" Juanito pleaded.

CLACKETY - CLACK! The train lurched into motion. Ungér stumbled again as Paulo slithered in the train behind Juanito and the loading plank fell to the ground.

"We can't leave Ungér!" Juanito pled. Paulo eyed the approaching trucks and Ungér …. The train was moving away quicker then Ungér was catching up.

Paulo shocked them both by wrapping his long tail around Ungér's front legs trying to drag her onto the train. Their powerful slinky body seemed to stretch beyond its limits until finally Ungér's front two legs were in the open boxcar door. Her rear legs, peddling as fast as she could trying to get on board. Juanito moved over to help by bracing himself and pushing Ungér's body with his snout to help Paulo… Finally, Ungér tumbled in the boxcar, just out of the reach of Lorenzo and his men as Paulo used their mighty tail to slam the boxcar door shut.

Lorenzo, Santiago and the others ran as fast as they could pursuing the train… but could not catch up. Lorenzo pushed Santiago aside and tossed his silver lined gaucho hat in anger towards the departing boxcar.

“How can this pig be so lucky? Why do these other creatures join him?” Lorenzo complained. Santiago just smiled as the train crisscrossed among many others leaving the yard, making it impossible to tell which one Juanito and the others were on. Train whistles echoed from all directions, distracting Lorenzo even more. Juanito’s, Ungér’s, and Paulo’s train pulled farther away into the early evening, the first stars flickering above—leaving Lorenzo even farther behind…

Juanito and Ungér watched the southern Brazilian landscape roll through a crack in the boxcar’s door. Ungér cuddled into some cool straw to nurse the scrapes and deep scratches on her underside from being dragged onto the boxcar by Paulo. As they got farther away, Paulo slid over and opened the boxcar door so they could see out even better.

Grazing cattle dotted the lush pampas, where the fading jungle stretched into the distance. Above them, the stars danced in the clear night sky… more numerous than they had ever seen.

Paulo gazed at the fading Brazilian terrain on the horizon. “I made my way south because of the destruction that is going on in my home deeper in the Amazon.” Paulo eyed

Juanito and Ungér. "But somehow, I think helping you will help with that," Paulo nodded.

"The diverse countryside is beautiful," Ungér whispered, her wool glowing silver in the moonlight. "In Armenia we have a saying… 'all riches come from the earth'…" Ungér uttered.

"You are so right, Ungér. Unfortunately, you only see what's left… what they didn't take," Paulo hissed.

Juanito listened while Ungér faithfully followed along. Yes, she would follow this massive Iberian pig, this Juanito. Her confidence confused Juanito. "Ungér, why do you stick with me? Why do you believe in me even with my selfish ways?"

Ungér smiled at Juanito. "We have another saying, Juanito: He who looks for a friend without a fault will never find one."

Ungér nuzzled him. "We are now friends, Juanito. My kind have wandered for generations, and we focus on our friend's loyalty and companionship, not their faults."

Juanito felt a warmth in his heart that had nothing to do with Ungér's woolly coat.

As dawn broke over the train the next morning, they could see the lush wetlands of the *Pantanal* on the eastern horizon. It was a tapestry of water, grass and blue sky. Where water receded near cracks in muddy shallows, steam rose up and drifted over purple and pink wildflowers.

The train chugged along and moved into northern Bolivia, and they found themselves in the wetlands of *Llanos de Moxos*. They were startled by flocks of *Blue-throated colorful Macaw* parrots that fluttered between trees and the piercing, cackling conversations they shared with each other. The air hummed with insect life and the faint smell of all the animal life around them…

When the train slowed to a crawl to cross a rickety bridge, they made their escape…

No sooner had they caught their breath than they heard the engines roar. Lorenzo, relentless in his pursuit, had somehow picked up their trail again.

"How does he keep finding us?" Juanito wondered aloud.

Paulo's keen eyes spotted something. "There! On your ear, Juanito. It is a tracking device!" Juanito shook his head. "I thought it was just to count me. So, they knew who I was."

Ungér smiled at Juanito. “By now, everyone on this continent knows who Juanito is; the behemoth Iberian pig.”

As they worked to remove the tiny tag, Ungér had an idea. “We should head to *Peru*,” she suggested. “It's not the direct route, but it might throw Lorenzo off our trail.”

Juanito hesitated. “But that will take so much longer, won’t it?”

Ungér sighed and moved closer to Juanito.

“Sometimes, the longest way around is the shortest way home. Trust me, Juanito. This is how my kind have survived through the worst of times.”

Paulo nodded. “Your friend is wise, Juanito. I know these wetlands. I can guide you through.”

Paulo told them stories of the Pantanal's diverse ecosystem. They spoke of jaguars that swam like fish, of trees that walked, and of fish that could breathe air. Whether any of it was true or not was not important. It was the warm friendship that meant everything to them.

"Everything is connected," Paulo explained. "Just as I learn to connect with myself, who I really am, we must learn to see the connections in nature."

Their journey was fraught with danger. But Paulo helped them through it. On the first few days of their trek together, a *caiman,* that South American cousin to the alligator, snapped as Juanito got a bit too close to a river's edge.

"Be alert, Juanito. You are a tasty feast to more than just humans," Paulo warned. The colorful boa constrictor then slithered over to a pile of cut cedar tree logs and pushed them in the water to block the reptile beast from partaking of Juanito.

"Thank you, Paulo, I owe you one." Juanito smiled at them. Sure enough, in the next clearing Juanito stepped in front of Paulo, impeding their progress.

"What is it, Juanito?" Ungér asked. Juanito pushed a rather large rock with his snout over to what looked like more land.

KERPLUNK! The rock quickly sank into loose wet sand that appeared to swallow the rock.

"Yikes! Quicksand!" Paulo exclaimed. "I would have sunk straight in if you didn't warn me, Juanito," Paulo hissed.

"Well, aren't you the careful one, Juanito," Ungér smiled.

"When you are as low to the ground as I am… always on the lookout for food, I notice these sorts of things," Juanito proudly stated.

Paulo smiled at Juanito and hissed their approval. "Thank you Juanito. For your thoughtful act, please follow me over here." Paulo led Juanito and Ungér to a large palm type tree. At the base ripe, purple *acai* berries had fallen from the high branches. Ungér and Juanito devoured them.

A coconut shaped pod crashed down from a nearby nut tree, spilling *Brazil nuts* across the ground. Juanito rushed to claim them all, while Ungér just shook her head as Juanito once again returned to his selfish ways. Ungér just sighed and continued to partake of the acai berries.

That evening, as they rested by a peaceful lagoon, Paulo turned to Juanito and Ungér. "You know, I've never felt so accepted. With you, I can just be myself."

Ungér smiled. "And we're glad for it, Paulo. Your uniqueness has saved us more than once."

Juanito nodded in agreement. “I'm grateful for this adventure. It's shown me the value of friendship and being true to oneself.”

The trio felt a sense of peace as the sun set over the far, distant Pantanal, painting the sky in vibrant oranges and purples. The diverse wildlife roamed among the tropical vegetation, while a colorful *Jabiru Stork* flapped its large wings in the rising moonlight, its beautiful white plumage below its black head and lower bright red neck.

The weary travelers knew the road ahead would be challenging, but they felt ready to face whatever came their way together.

“I have hitched a ride on many of these trains. I know which ones can get us to the north, even if we take a detour or two,” Paulo hissed.

As they journeyed on, they carried with them not just their hopes for the future but the strength they had found in each other's differences and the unbreakable bond of their friendship…

Chapter 4:
The Lost Jungle

Acorn of wisdom:

The Amazon Rainforest produces about 20% of the world's oxygen and is often called "The Lungs of the Earth."

As they left any memories of Argentina, Paraguay, and Brazil behind, the three journey mates trudged through Bolivia towards Peru. The morning dew clung heavy on Paulo's scales as Juanito and Ungér followed the slithering boa on the jungle path. Paulo's colorful body wound gracefully between weathered fence posts carved into farmland. An urgency in their eyes had them moving faster than ever, leaving Juanito struggling to keep up.

"I have never seen a snake of your size travel so fast, Paulo," Ungér commented.

"Watch your step," Paulo warned, their voice carrying an edge of bitterness. "The ground isn't as stable as it used to be. What they are doing deeper in the Amazon is now happening here too."

Juanito, still adjusting to life on the run, grumbled as his hooves sank into the muddy earth. "I don't see why we couldn't take the road. My hooves weren't made for this terrain."

"Because the road is where they'll look for us first," Ungér reminded him gently. She picked her way carefully across the unstable ground.

The sky became dark, and it seemed like the sun itself had left the sky. They eyed each other with a confused look.

Suddenly, a distant roar; unlike anything they had ever heard, rumbled through the jungle. They froze in their tracks. Paulo raised their head as they tasted the air with a flick of their tongue.

"Do you smell that?" Paulo nervously asked.

Juanito sniffed, his sensitive nose twitching. "Smoke?"

As they all turned around, flames roared toward them. A wild, fiery blaze was upon them in seconds. The crackle of the raging inferno engulfed the massive kapok trees. The intense heat herded Juanito and Ungér inside of a circle of dancing orange and bright blue flames. Paulo was at a lost of what to do… They just coiled up and hissed.

CRASH! … CRASH! ... CRASH!

The fiery remains of nearby kapok trees came crashing down.

"Run!" Juanito screamed. But there was no way to escape the circle.

It was as if the jungle itself was on fire and after all three journey mates.

CRASH!

Juanito barely scrambled out of the way of a fiery, falling tree branch. He dodged burning embers, and they were engulfed in smoke.

WOOSH!

The flames that encircled Juanito and Ungér parted just a bit.

"This way," coughed Ungér.

An acrid, wet smoke swirled above them.

"That smells horrible," Juanito lamented.

But then Paulo took charge.

"Follow me! They are burning the rubber trees also, anything in their way," Paulo hissed. They followed Paulo into a shallow stream with just their eyes above the water level to watch the fire burn itself around them…

Finally… the flames passed by as they stayed in the water.

Paulo slithered up a fallen log for a better view, their wet scales gleaming in the early morning light that fought its way through the dense smoke. In the distance, while the fire was gone, columns of dark smoke rose above what was left of a charred tree line. Paulo gestured for Juanito and Ungér to leave the stream and join them.

"The same thing is happening here as what is happening to my home deep in the Amazon," Paulo continued, their eyes distant. "The canopy used to be so thick you could barely see the sky." They gestured with their tail at the patchwork of burnt, cleared land around them.

"Why do they burn and remove so much of what is here?" Ungér asked softly, though she suspected she already knew the answer.

"Progress," Paulo spat the word like it was poison. "That is what they called it when they came with their machines. First it was just a few trees, then more... Then whole sections of the forest disappeared overnight. Families were separated, or worse... gone."

Juanito shifted uncomfortably. The old Juanito would have dismissed Paulo's story as irrelevant to his own concerns. But something had changed in Juanito since he left the Dehesa. "And your family?" he asked quietly.

Paulo's misty eyes widened slightly at Juanito's unexpected empathy.

"As I said, we boa constrictors don't really have families. But there were many other animals in my rainforest too. I did enjoy watching them and hearing their sounds every morning until the noise of the destruction started. Unfortunately, many of those animals scattered or worse, didn't make it."

Paulo slithered back and forth eyeing the burnt horizon, upset.

"So many have lost so much. Where do they expect us to go?" Paulo lamented.

Ungér pressed close to Paulo for comfort, while Juanito found himself blinking back unexpected tears. "I'm so sorry, Paulo. I had no idea."

"Few do," Paulo replied. "It's easier to ignore the cost of progress when you don't see who pays the price." They started moving again, leading them through a narrow gap between two agricultural fields. "I thought I could escape it all. But you can't run forever."

Their banter was interrupted by the rumble of approaching vehicles.

"Don't let them see us! Follow me!" Paulo hissed.

Paulo quickly ushered them into a dense thicket of surviving jungle growth. They watched as a convoy of logging trucks passed by on a nearby dirt road, their beds loaded with freshly cut timber.

On the side of the trucks, the same logo that was on Santiago's name tag when Juanito first met him… the fancy golden lettering of Lorenzo Valdez Enterprises…

"Lorenzo's family business is everywhere," Paulo whispered. "What they don't cut down, they burn and sell the cleared land to the highest bidder."

As they waited for the trucks to pass, a small group of displaced animals emerged from the undergrowth; a family of *howler monkeys* and colorful birds scattered. Juanito hid behind a tree as a small herd of *tapirs* came rumbling by. They looked like a cross between an elephant and a pig with a noticeably short trunk. They were thin and confused, their homes destroyed by the recent clearing.

Paulo slithered forward, urging them to safety…

"Pssst! My wayward friends, over here!" Paulo hissed. The animals all froze in place. They eyed Juanito and Ungér and were totally confused. Animals were usually a little leery of others in the Amazon. They were especially confused to see the massive Juanito.

"You can hide with us! Hurry before it's too late," Juanito whispered.

The tapirs and the howler monkeys did a double take, but the oncoming trucks scared them even more.

VROOM! The rev of the truck engines made their decision for them… they jumped into what was left of the underbrush and hid with Ungér, Juanito and Paulo.

Without hesitation, Ungér approached all the different animals. “Are you alright? Do you need help?”

One of the howler monkeys, whose name was Mona, clutched her baby close. “We don't know where to go. Our home, it's just gone,” Mona sobbed. Ungér noticed the baby monkey was covered with the black soot residue of smoke. Ungér nuzzled Mona towards the clear stream.

“Come, follow me,” Ungér insisted.

As everyone watched with bated breath…

Ungér led Mona, who held her baby to her chest, into the stream. Ungér nodded to Mona to rinse her young, frightened offspring in the cool water. Mona carefully rinsed the youngling off, scooping water with her tiny hands.

As she pulled her clean infant monkey out of the water, the wooly Ungér pushed up against the wet baby monkey in Mona's arms and used her wool to dry off the young one.

SQUEAK! SQUAK! COO! The clean, happy baby cuddled into the wool of Ungér, who nodded 'you're welcome' with moist eyes… Paulo, Juanito and the tapirs all looked at the affectionate moment with their own moist eyes…

The action moved Mona to full tears.

"Thank you. You are so kind to use your fleece for my baby," Mona uttered. The words moved Ungér. But she had to turn away. It broke her heart to see them in such a crisis.

Juanito studied the displaced animals and confusion filled his face. Juanito, who was so used to being in his own world, was being affected by the plight of so many others…. Something very foreign to him.

To everyone's surprise, including himself, Juanito spoke up next. "Come with us," he said, stepping forward. "We're heading north, to a place called The River of Nueces. There's supposed to be room for everyone there."

Paulo and Ungér exchanged amazed glances at Juanito's offer. The displaced animals looked tempted but ultimately shook their heads.

"This is our land," Mona said. "Changed as it is, we have to find a way to survive here. But thank you for offering." The tapirs nodded in agreement.

Mona and her offspring fell in line behind the tapirs.

"Yes, we must find a way to survive… we must," Mona sobbed as she squeezed her baby.

Her words struck Paulo deeply… they all were staying while Paulo was leaving. Still, Paulo slithered over behind Juanito, committed to their journey north.

Paulo slithered back and forth. An internal conflict brewing.

"What is it Paulo? Is there more danger near?"

"No, I just think how brave she is; braver than I am," Paulo whispered. "I'm leaving… and yet she is staying. So are the others."

Ungér and Juanito were at a loss for words.

As the group of displaced animals disappeared back into what remained of the burnt jungle, Juanito watched them go with troubled eyes. "I never understood before," he said quietly. "Back on the Dehesa, when the oak tree disease came, I just thought about how it affected me. I never considered how many others were suffering too."

Paulo slithered closer. "Understanding is the first step toward change, my friend. And you have changed more than you know."

But as Paulo said the words, they seemed to affect the colorful snake. As if there was a hidden truth in them. As if Paulo were missing something. As they went on their way, Paulo hesitated and just watched the diminished glow of the flame-ravaged rainforest behind them. Paulo then looked to the path where the tapirs and howler monkeys went. Paulo kept thinking … *I am leaving... yet they are staying…* Paulo slowly serpentined their way to catch up to Juanito and Ungér.

They all spent that night sheltered in the hollow of a massive dead kapok tree, one of the few remaining giants from the old forest.

Juanito watched Paulo coil comfortably on a fallen log. Something had been bothering Juanito about Paulo's behavior.

"Paulo, I noticed you never share the fruits and vegetables we find. Don't you get hungry?"

Paulo's scales shimmered in the filtered moonlight. "Ah, I prefer to dine privately. And I can go weeks, sometimes over a month without eating. It's how we boas are made."

Juanito seemed relieved, though slightly puzzled, by this explanation.

"Uh, what do you mean?" Juanito asked.

"Believe me, you do not want to know, Juanito," Ungér nodded in understanding. "Paulo dines on other things besides fruits and vegetables."

The conversation drifted to other matters as the jungle hummed around them.

"Are you all right?" Ungér asked Paulo softly.

Paulo was still struggling with seeing the heartache of the animals affected by the fires in their beloved Amazon. "I've been so focused on what was lost, I almost missed what could be gained, helping others." Juanito oinked and nodded his head in agreement.

As they resumed their journey toward Peru, the smoking columns behind them cast long shadows in the setting sun. But ahead, the first stars were beginning to appear, pointing the way forward. Clusters of palm trees stood like slender sentinels guarding the remains of a once lush kingdom. As they stopped for the night, Paulo just eyed where they had come from, then looked north.

"Do you think it really exists?" Paulo asked.

Juanito replied with unexpected conviction. "It must exist not only for us… but for those who need a place to belong."

Ungér nodded in agreement. "We should make sure it's a place where everyone is welcome."

Paulo looked between their two friends. They had lost so much, but in these unlikely companions, they had found something precious… hope.

The next morning, they continued their journey toward Peru, carrying with them not just their own dreams, but the hopes of all those they'd met along the way. The path ahead would be challenging, but together, they were stronger than they'd ever been alone…

Chapter 5: Ice-Covered Peaks, and a Warm-Hearted Woman

Acorn of wisdom:

The Andes Mountains stretch through seven countries and are the longest mountain range in the world.

In Peru, the frigid wind in the *Andes* howled, whipping snow and ice around the group of travelers. Paulo, the colorful boa constrictor that they were, appeared so out of place in the snow. But their beautiful rainbow silhouette shined even brighter against nature's white backdrop. They slithered through the snow with surprising ease, their cold-blooded nature adapting to the harsh environment.

“I thought snakes did not like the cold?” Ungér wondered.

Paulo coiled up as if ready to strike.

“Thinking about that... that... Lorenzo Valdez makes my blood boil,” Paulo hissed. “It is like the flames we saw from where we just came, burn inside of me,” Paulo uttered as they shuddered to keep warm.

WOOOOOOSH!

A large chunk of snow came crashing down on the three, covering them all up. It was if they were gone… For a moment there was silence… then Paulo’s head came slithering out of the bright white mound on the skinny mountain path. Frantic, Paulo pushed as much snow away as they could… finally, Ungér’s head appeared. Typical Ungér, she was only concerned about others… specifically, Juanito.

“Help me dig Paulo! Juanito! We must save Juanito!” she screamed.

The two of them scrapped and nuzzled the snow… nothing! Just when all hope seemed to wane… the behemoth Juanito’s massive head appeared.

He shivered and complained, unaware he almost met his demise.

“I told you this was a bad idea!” he snorted. “I was almost turned into a pork popsicle!” Ungér smiled at Paulo then at Juanito.

“Uh, I don’t think there would be much of a demand for those,” Ungér laughed. But Juanito was not amused. His frustration with the cold was showing.

Juanito, the once-proud Iberian pig, was struggling. Even with the layers of insulation of his pork padding, he shivered uncontrollably.

“I… I cannot… go on,” Juanito stammered, his enormous frame shivering. “This is too much of a detour. Maybe... maybe we should turn back. Find somewhere warmer.”

Ungér pressed close to him, her thick wool offering what little warmth she could. “Don't give up, Juanito. We've come too far to stop now.”

“But it's so cold!” Juanito whined, his selfish instincts surfacing. “Why should I suffer like this? I was meant for sunny meadows and acorn feasts, not this icy nightmare!”

Ungér smiled and leaned into him.

"Oh, stop whining. Look on the bright side… if we get stuck here, at least you'll be a well-preserved ham for some future archaeologist to discover."

"Whining? Some of us are not adorned with nature's wool blanket!"

The sarcastic comment caught Ungér off-guard. "Is that all you can think about? Your comfort?" She stepped back, fixated on Juanito with a hard stare. "Do you think any of us were meant for this? Look at Paulo. A boa constrictor in the Andes? That shouldn't be possible. But they are determined. And do you think I dreamed of trudging through the snow as a lamb?"

Juanito, taken aback by her outburst, fell silent.

Ungér sighed, her voice softening. "Juanito, there's something I never told you. About how I ended up in that slaughterhouse."

The group huddled closer, seeking shelter behind a large boulder as Ungér began her tale.

"My flock was a rare wild flock. We did not belong to any ranch. We were being pursued by poachers in the mountains of Argentina. We were exhausted, and they were closing in. I knew someone had to create a diversion, or we'd all be captured." Her eyes grew distant with the memory. "So, I let myself get caught in a bramble bush, bleating loudly to draw their attention. The rest of the flock escaped, but I was snagged."

Juanito's eyes widened in understanding. "So, you weren't separated in the port. You sacrificed yourself for them?" Juanito became reflective. Hearing how Ungér was so heroic, it reminded him how he wasn't.

"I didn't always live on the Dehesa," Juanito shivered. "I was born on a small farm. The biggest pig they had ever seen. But I quickly ate more than my fair share."

Juanito slumped to the ground. He slowly raised his head to Ungér and then Paulo. He hesitated but then opened up to them both.

"One day, Señor García came to take me. I fought, squealed, and dug my hooves in. I wanted to stay with my family, my brother and sister. I didn't care that I ate more than my share of the food. Why did I have to leave? Why me?"

The silence was only broken by the sound of Juanito's shivering and chattering teeth. He noticed Ungér was in deep thought. She then raised her head and measured her words to make sure she said exactly what she wanted to say to Juanito.

"Maybe…." She began. She eyed Juanito up and down.

"Maybe by you leaving, you saved your brother and sister. They would now have enough to eat." Paulo and Ungér eyed the embarrassed Juanito.

Juanito paused and stared at the ground. He then raised his eyes to Ungér. The words she spoke to him rocked him back as he contemplated the powerful sentiment of his unintended sacrifice so long ago.

"I uh, I never even thought about that," Juanito muttered.

Ungér moved closer to Juanito and looked him in the eyes. "Sometimes, you must do what's best for others, not just yourself. That's what it means to be part of a flock, or a family."

The weight of her words hung heavy in the icy air. Juanito felt a sorrow creep over him thinking about his brother and sister.

This journey was proving more than Juanito bargained for. The Dehesa had been everything to him… or so he thought. But now he wondered if he'd been happy there simply because the endless acorns let him forget his past, forget his brother and sister. Only Conejo had made it truly feel like home.

Juanito eyed Ungér as she plowed through the snow. Ungér turned around to make sure Juanito was okay.

"Follow my steps Juanito, I will push the snow away, so it is easier for you," Ungér encouraged him.

Why was she so nice to him when he kept complaining? Yes, Ungér was special. Paulo slithered in front of him to push the snow even farther away. Juanito just stopped… eyeing them both. He was amazed that a boa constrictor could survive in such cold. And the delicate Ungér, whose spirit was hardened by her commitment to her friends defied logic. Then it hit Juanito. They did it because they believed in

Juanito. His dream was now their dream. Both Ungér and Paulo turned around to see why Juanito had stopped.

"Juanito, do you need us to stop behind that boulder?" Ungér asked.

"Just let us know Juanito," Paulo hissed. "We can slow down…"

Juanito teared up at their support, but the cold quickly turned them into ice crystals. Just when Juanito thought he couldn't go on, Ungér yelled out.

"Look!" she exclaimed, gesturing with her head. "There's a village just ahead! We might find help there."

They could make out the faint outlines of small, sturdy rock huts through the swirling snow. The blizzard began to subside as they approached the remote settlement, revealing a quiet, rugged yet beautiful scene.

The village was a cluster of stone structures built to withstand the harsh mountain climate. Smoke curled from chimneys, and colorful prayer flags fluttered in the wind. Outside one of the smaller huts sat an older woman, Chaska; her weathered hands working a loom with practiced ease.

Chaska seemed surprised as she spotted the unusual group. Her dark eyes, bright with intelligence, took in the shivering pig, the determined sheep, and the graceful snake. She sensed there was something special about this high-altitude motley group as soon as she saw them.

"Come, wandering friends, come closer," Chaska implored them.

Paulo slithered in front of the group, cautious of the lady.

"Don't be afraid. You are welcome here. This is a very welcoming village," she insisted.

Ungér, seeing Juanito's terrible condition, had an idea. She approached Chaska, bleating softly and rubbing against her, then moved to Juanito and back again.

Chaska's eyes widened in understanding. "Ah," she said, her voice warm and rich. "You want me to help your friend?"

Paulo, ever cautious, whispered. "We don't have time for this. Lorenzo could be right behind us. We need to keep moving."

Ungér stood her ground. “No, Paulo. We can't leave Juanito like this. He will die from this cold. We're all in this together, remember?”

As they debated, Chaska had already begun to work. Her gnarled but nimble fingers snipped some of Ungér's wool. She bypassed washing it because of the extreme cold. But she brushed the wool fibers repeatedly, spinning them into smooth rolls of yarn.

Ungér pushed up against Juanito, who still was shivering with the cold. Paulo coiled up and blocked a cold breeze that attacked Juanito’s backside. Chaska smiled at how the three of them huddled so close together to help Juanito stay warm. A few other villagers peeked out of their rock huts but stayed inside. Chaska moved back and forth in the labor of love gathering everything together to prepare Juanito’s garment to be while the three just sat and watched her every move.

She quickly dyed and dried the yarn in assorted colors. They all listened to the sound of the clicking of the loom as Chaska wove Ungér's wool into something new. “Ungér,” Juanito said, his voice thick with emotion, “you're giving up your wool for me? Even after how I have acted?”

Ungér nuzzled him. “Of course, Juanito. That is what friends do. That's what family does.” Juanito bristled at her affection. But then he smiled and leaned into her. They both seemed surprised by their spontaneous acts… but enjoyed it.

With help from Paulo and Ungér, Chaska draped the warm garment over Juanito's bulky frame. The pig sighed in relief as warmth seeped into his bones.

Ungér marveled at how pretty the colorful sweater looked. There were row after row of tiny story blocks all connected together. The design told a tale of mountains and valleys, of hardship and triumph.

“Shat sirun es!” Ungér blurted out.

Juanito and Paulo seemed confused.

“It means, 'you are beautiful’ in Armenian,” Ungér clarified.

“No one has ever called me beautiful before,” an embarrassed Juanito responded.

Ungér giggled. “Don't let it go to your head. My wool in the sweater helps, too.”

"Thank you," Juanito said, addressing Chaska and Ungér. His eyes welled with tears. "I... I do not know what to say." Juanito pushed a bit of firewood into the fire. He pushed all the scraps of Ungér's wool into a neat pile for Chaska.

"Why thank you," Chaska uttered with surprise. Ungér and Paulo eyed each other at Juanito's kind gesture.

"I have been so selfish, so focused on my discomfort. You've all shown me what true kindness and sacrifice looks like," Juanito declared.

Chaska smiled. Patting Juanito's now-covered back, her eyes twinkled as she spoke. "No need for words, young one. Kindness speaks for itself. And it seems you have much to learn from your friends."

"How do you speak our language?" Ungér asked.

"It is not your language, child, it is the language of kindness," she smiled.

She reached up and touched the sweater she made for Juanito. "You see these small patterns? Each one tells a story through unity. Like these spirals, they represent how life keeps moving forward, even when the path seems to circle back on itself."

Juanito studied the design with new appreciation. Everything on their journey suddenly seemed more connected, more purposeful. And to Juanito it seemed like some of their journey appeared on the sweater too. But he was quickly distracted. Ungér and Paulo prepared to leave. Chaska pressed a small pouch into Ungér's wool. “Moist herbs,” she explained. “They will quench any doubt when you need it most.”

But Chaska eyed the darkening sky. She insisted they stay for the night. “The mountain passes are treacherous in the dark,” she warned them.

Inside her rock walled home, the walls were covered with tapestries telling stories of mountain life. Juanito, wrapped in his new sweater, studied them. One weaving caught his eye… it showed various animals working together to survive a great storm. A small group of Andean fox species called *culpeo,* were huddled together in a tight circle. They look like a reddish-gray fur pinwheel as they cuddled together for warmth.

“That was a winter when I was still a child, before I came to live in these mountains,” Chaska explained. “When the snows came early and stayed late. Back then I lived down in the nearby valley. My people observed the wild creatures that lived up in these mountains. We noticed how they worked together to get through the worst of times. They taught us about unity." She couldn't take her eyes off the tapestry of the foxes. Neither could Juanito or Ungér.

Chaska stirred a pot of herbal tea and put some in shallow earthen pots for Juanito and Ungér to enjoy. The aroma filled the dark space except for the flicker of a small fire whose smoke escaped through a skinny opening in the rock ceiling.

Paulo slithered closer to the warmth of the stone hearth. "I still don't understand how you can speak with animals?" Curiosity was evident in their voice.

Chaska smiled, her wrinkles deepening. "As I said, that understanding comes with the gift of kindness. A gift I unexpectedly received after a very dark time in my life. I lost a child in childbirth and could have no other."

Chaska sipped her tea as the steam from her cup moved past her moist eyes. She sighed and continued her story.

"Then I lost my husband and our farm to those who wanted it. I felt there was no reason to go on. The people from these mountains traded with our farm for years, I knew them well. When I had no place to go… they took me in." She stared at the different tapestries, each one with different animals.

"The animals of these mountains always would stay next to me when I worked harvesting potatoes," she reminisced. "It was as if they wanted me to understand they were there for me. That they understood my loss; as they had suffered losses. So, they spoke to me with their kindness--" she stopped, moist eyed.

"Potatoes? Yum!" Juanito interrupted. Ungér glared at him.

"Sorry," Juanito lowered his head. Chaska was glad Juanito changed the subject. She regained her composure.

"Yes, potatoes. These mountains are the birthplace of potatoes. The first one appeared here thousands of years ago. Our most prized food," she eyed Juanito.

"I never knew where potatoes were from. I just ate them when I could," Juanito smiled.

"There's a lot you don't know, Juanito," Ungér smiled. "But stop interrupting, let her finish," Ungér implored.

Chaska opened a full-length wool flap-like door. She nodded toward all the other rock huts that had smoke coming out of their chimneys.

"As I was saying, these people took me in. They became my new family. They showed me that even if we lose everything, we must go on to find what is important."

Chaska just smiled at them.

"Help others when they need help. When they have no place to go."

Ungér spoke up. "Like my flock," she said softly. "I lost them… to save them."

"And gained new friends in return," Chaska nodded, gesturing to Juanito and Paulo.

"So, what do you feel is <u>the</u> most important thing we need on the rest of our journey? Courage, persistence? What do you think, wise woman?" Juanito asked.

Chaska looked them each in the eye, then smiled…

"Kindness."

Nothing else had to be said. They all felt the warmth between them all.

The wind howled outside, but inside the hut, stories flowed as freely as the tea. Chaska shared tales of the mountains; of ancient paths known only to the vicuñas, of hidden valleys where rare herbs grew, of caves that could shelter travelers from the fiercest storms.

"I will tell you of a path that will get you to the north. The animals showed it to me when I first came here. So, I could sneak down to the valley to grab crops from an unguarded field of my old farm that was stolen from me," she confidently spoke.

Chaska opened her wool door again as the blizzard subsided; pointed to a very obscure path. "Tomorrow," she said, "you must take the eastern path. It is longer but safer. The western trail may seem more direct, but it leads through territory controlled by poachers and far worse things. Men who work with men like this Lorenzo you mentioned."

Juanito shifted uncomfortably. "But the eastern path will take us farther away from our destination," he protested, old selfish habits dying hard.

Chaska fixated on him with a knowing look. "Young pig, you wear a sweater made from your friend's wool. Would you rather be warm and alive on a longer path, or frozen on a shorter one?"

Ungér could not resist. "Juanito, sometimes, the longest way around is the shortest way, remember?"

Juanito lowered his head, properly chastised. "You are right. I apologize."

Later that night, as Ungér and Paulo slept, Juanito remained awake, watching the fire's dying embers. Chaska sat beside him, her weathered hands working on another small project.

"Something troubles you," she said. It was not a question.

Juanito squirmed, not really wanting to talk about it. He changed the subject.

"Chaska? That is a different name," Juanito whispered. Chaska poked the fire to make the embers flare up. She put another piece of wood in the flames.

"Chaska means star in my native language, *Quechua.* It also means guidance and kindness," she smiled.

"Guidance? That is interesting. I think that is what I need," Juanito whispered.

Chaska studied Juanito. "You speak of guidance as to what lies in front of you. But I think the look in your eyes reveal you think of where you came from," she surmised.

"It has been a hard journey," Juanito agreed.

Chaska smiled and shook her head. "I am not talking of your trek. I am talking about what you left behind."

Juanito teared up. He was surprised how Chaska could know what he was thinking. In a whispering voice Juanito opened up to Chaska.

"I left my brother and sister and my best friend Conejo… and I think about them all the time. Well, not my brother and sister so much, but Conejo and I were so close, and I left him. I left all of them."

Chaska raised up Juanito's snout to look him straight in the eyes.

"You did not leave anyone, Juanito. You were put on this journey for a reason. There was nothing else you could do for those you left behind," Chaska stated. "It was meant for you to move on, to be here at this very moment in time."

The words seemed to soak into Juanito. He stared over at Ungér and Paulo who were sleeping. He gestured for Chaska to come closer…

Chaska scooted closer so Juanito could whisper in her ear.

"I'm afraid," Juanito admitted, his voice barely a whisper. "Afraid of failing them. What if The River of Nueces does not exist? What if I am leading them nowhere? What if this dream is unreachable?"

Chaska's hands stilled. "Dreams are like these mountains, young one. From a distance, they seem impossible to cross. But you take one step, then another, and suddenly you find yourself on the other side." Chaska counseled him.

"But what about Ungér's dream of finding a flock? And Paulo's hope for a safe home? I feel selfish for dragging them along on my quest."

Chaska shook her head. "Look at what you're wearing. Your friend's wool keeps you warm. In return, your strength and size help protect them. Paulo's wisdom guides you all. You're not dragging them anywhere. You are all carrying each other. This is destiny; a destiny for all of you," Chaska wisely uttered.

Juanito felt a little bit better hearing Chaska's perspective. He fell asleep as the fire crackled in the middle of them, the sound of her words tapering off, but their meaning now embedded in his heart.

Dawn broke over the mountains, painting the snow in shades of pink and gold. Chaska stood in her doorway as the trio prepared to leave, their spirits renewed by rest and wisdom.

She handed them a crude cloth sack. "Here is some *chuño,* dried potatoes that will keep well on your trip. They will last you at least through *Colombia.*"

Juanito's eyes begged for a sample. Chaska noticed and she reached in the bag and fed one to Juanito. Juanito chewed it and his eyes let her know he wanted another one.

"No, Juanito, they must last you and Ungér for quite a while," Chaska insisted as she sent them on their way. She secured the bag of dried potatoes to Juanito's sweater, but maybe a bit too close to his chin.

“Remember,” she called after them, “the eastern path. Follow the rising sun, and trust in each other.”

As they made their way down the snowy trail, Juanito felt different. The sweater warmed his body, but it was Chaska's words that had warmed his heart. He looked at his friends. Ungér, with her shortened but still thick wool, and Paulo, who moved with surprising grace through the snow. Juanito felt a surge of gratitude.

“Thank you,” Juanito said suddenly, stopping in his tracks.

“For what?” Ungér asked.

“For everything. For being here. For believing in me even when I didn't believe in myself.” He touched Ungér’s wool with his snout. “I promise to be worthy of your friendship.”

Paulo smiled. “You already are ‘mi amigo.’ Now, shall we find this River of Nueces?”

The group now faced the daunting task of navigating the unknown mountain passes to continue their journey north. But the cold and the twisting path confused them. As they came to a fork in the path, Juanito sneaked a bite of one of the dried potato snacks in the bag that draped near his chin.

Distracted, he took the western path… not the eastern one as Chaska had told him. Ungér and Paulo, who were weary from navigating the difficult path, followed and didn't notice that Juanito had taken the wrong path either.

Chapter 6:

A Winged Warrior Joins the Journey

Acorn of wisdom:

Andean condors can soar for hours without flapping their wings once, using warm air currents to glide.

As they came out of one of the mountain passes, a shadow passed overhead. They looked up to see an enormous Andean condor circling above them. It was breathtaking, and its keen eyes seemed to pierce right through them. It was a massive bird with a wingspan of over ten feet. Its feathers were a jet-black color with a ruffle of snow-white feathers encircling its neck. Its head was a combination of a pink and dark red color.

“Be careful,” Paulo hissed. “Condors aren't known for their friendliness.”

The condor swooped lower, and the group braced themselves for an attack. But instead, the condor landed on a boulder above them, tilting its head, speaking without hesitation.

“What brings such an unusual group to these heights?”

Ungér, ever the diplomat, stepped forward. “I'm Ungér, and these are my friends Juanito and Paulo. We're on a journey away from those who would harm us, to a place where animals can be free and safe.”

The condor looked back at the path they had come from out of the Andes mountains.

“You have taken the wrong path. You should have gone east. It is safer,” the condor nodded.

“We did take the eastern path. Uh, at least I thought we did,” Juanito responded. Juanito braced for complaints from his traveling partners.

“Juanito, when you lead there is a responsibility,” Ungér stated.

Juanito looked down at the remaining dried potatoes in the sack around his chin. "I will make it up to you somehow," he promised Ungér.

Paulo didn't like Ungér being disappointed at Juanito.

"No worries, Juanito. We still can find our better life," Paulo hissed.

The condor's eyes softened at the exchange. "I'm Zephyr. And I understand more than you might think about seeking a better life."

In the distance a small group of condors flew together… two juvenile birds new to flight, struggled to keep up. The mini flock flew closer to Zephyr. It seemed like the adult condors shook their heads in disappointment at Zephyr; the condors banked and flew away with their young offspring in their shadows…

Zephyr sighed at their departure but then focused on Juanito and Ungér. Zephyr's story was much like everyone's in the group. "I've always felt like an outsider," she confided, her wings rustling. "It took me a long time to accept that I didn't fit in with the other condors."

Juanito, intrigued, asked, “What do you mean fit in? We are all different in some way.”

Zephyr sighed, her massive wings drooping. “The other condors... they all paired off, built nests, laid eggs. I was expected to do the same; find a mate, to rear chicks, but it wasn’t... wasn’t for me.”

Paulo nodded. “I know that feeling all too well.”

“For the longest time, I thought something was wrong with me,” Zephyr continued. “The other condors would whisper, wondering why I never joined their mating rituals. But over time, I realized that my uniqueness wasn't a flaw.”

Ungér tilted her head. “How so?”

Zephyr's eyes gleamed. “While the others were busy with their nests, I was free to explore; to see the world from high above. I've seen things they could not imagine. And now, I use my perspective to help others, guide lost travelers, and spot dangers from afar.”

Juanito, moved by Zephyr's story, spoke up. “That's incredible, Zephyr. You found purpose in what others may call being different.”

"There is nothing I want more than to find a flock and be a mother," Ungér professed. "But I respect how you feel. Please, join us."

Zephyr eyed the other condors who were now a speck in the distance.

"My brethren are leaving with their offspring because of the strip mining of gold and copper in the Andes," Zephyr said with a tinge of sorrow. "You know what? I think I will join you in your quest. My wings and eyes could be useful on your journey," Zephyr exclaimed.

The group exchanged excited glances. Ungér spoke for them all: "We'd be honored to have you with us, Zephyr."

"We can all learn so much from each other. Our stories are so unique. But in many ways the same." Juanito declared. He broke out some of the dried potatoes and stingily shared them with whoever desired to partake.

Over the next week or two, Zephyr's aerial perspective proved invaluable as they navigated the jagged mountains. Zephyr swooped down and landed on a nearby rock as they came out of the mountains, and all of them gazed out at a spotted fertile valley.

"The train routes are less certain from here. But I will guide you the shortest way north. I will show you as the condor flies," she mused.

However, as they crossed Colombia, they found themselves in a new danger.

Zephyr, who circled above them for what seemed like hours at a time, swooped down and landed on a bare branch on a dead tree.

"By taking the western path rather than the eastern one, we will be passing through dangerous territory. I will keep an eye out, but this land is controlled by the cartels," Zephyr squawked.

"What are cartels?" Juanito asked.

"A group of men who make drugs from the plants that are harmful to so many," Zephyr sighed.

Vast fields of coca plants marred the lush landscapes, a stark reminder of those powerful cartels who owned them.

"This isn't right," Paulo said as their eyes scanned the destroyed natural habitats. "They're ruining the land harvesting these and using chemicals to make other drugs too."

Ungér nodded. "It's heartbreaking to see such beauty destroyed for greed. I know others in nearby countries are doing the same."

They passed by a coffee plantation and an orchard of cocoa bean trees.

Juanito, still wearing his Andean sweater, looked around. "We should keep moving. I have a bad feeling about this place. I wish I didn't take the wrong path."

Ungér noticed the cocoa beans and offered one of her fun facts.

"You know Juanito, chocolate, that sweet candy the humans eat, is made from these cocoa beans." Juanito just stared at the beans. He was confused.

"Actually, they are called 'cacao' beans," Zephyr explained. "But some do call them 'cocoa' beans. And yes, that is where chocolate comes from."

"So, there are 'coca' plants and 'cocoa' beans? Are they different?" Juanito asked.

"Way different," Zephyr chimed in. "You are a naïve one aren't you, Juanito?"

Ungér just smiled at Juanito. Zephyr had verbalized what she and Paulo already knew about Juanito. His worldly experience was limited to what he came across on this journey.

Juanito eyed the cocoa beans, defensive.

"Does not look like anything I would eat," he said. Juanito just trudged along. "But I am getting hungry," he stated. Ungér looked at the bag of dried potatoes on Juanito's sweater near his chin. There was a hole in the bag where Juanito had chewed through it. Juanito became embarrassed; he had eaten all the dried potatoes…

"Oh, Juanito, you ate all the chuno potatoes?" Ungér sighed. "That was supposed to last for many kilometers from here," Ungér shook her head. Juanito said the same thing again that he did after he had taken the wrong path earlier.

"Don't be mad at me, Ungér, I will make it up to you. I promise."

"I am not mad at you, Juanito… it is just who you are," Ungér uttered.

Juanito lowered his head, but was quickly distracted by something…

A farmer inside his farmhouse held a flyer up and looked out at Juanito, Ungér, Paulo and Zephyr flying overhead. The farmer kept looking at the flyer and then Juanito with concern.

Juanito's snout twitched, his eyes blinked rapidly.

"Why does that old man keep looking at me?" Juanito wondered.

"I wouldn't worry about him, Juanito, he's too old to catch you," Paulo interjected. Juanito's ears flicked back as if trying to shake off the feeling.

But the farmer kept looking at Juanito and the paper in his hand. He made Juanito feel uncomfortable. Juanito's stomach growled, and he belched nervously.

"Uh, excuse me," he apologized. Ungér eyed him and noticed his fidgety glare at the farmer in the window of the farmhouse.

"Don't worry, Juanito. He probably just never seen anything as big as you before," Ungér tried to reassure him.

Juanito eyed the farmer again in the window and just smiled at him. But the farmer stayed focused on Juanito with a scowl on his face… and then looked at the flyer once more. The way the farmer squinted at him, then back at the flyer, sent a chill down Juanito's spine.

"The sooner we are away from this area, the better I will feel," Juanito said.

The farmer in the farmhouse picked up his cell phone…

As the motley group continued their journey, they soon heard the roar of approaching vehicles. Juanito squinted and looked into the window of one of the distant crew cab trucks. He widened his eyes in disbelief. Lorenzo and Santiago were in the back seat.

"No! No way! How did he find us?" Juanito squealed. "We got rid of the tracker!"

Zephyr, flying above, signaled, and said, "That is a cartel vehicle!"

"Lorenzo knew we'd have to pass through Colombia eventually. He must have figured out you were heading north," Paulo surmised.

“But how?” Juanito wondered.

“It doesn’t matter, does it? He keeps coming,” Paulo hissed. They coiled together behind a bush, peering out at Lorenzo and the approaching cartel truck.

“I am sure Lorenzo contacted the cartels; told them to keep an eye out for us,” Paulo surmised. “Unfortunately, he is a very well-connected person.” Paulo hissed.

Juanito paced back and forth. “I don’t care how well connected he is. We went up into the Andes and he still could find us? I don’t believe it. Why am I so important?”

Ungér’s disbelief concurred with Juanito.

“Do you really think the cartel—those men who make and sell drugs around the world—care about Lorenzo’s quest to find some wayward pig?” Ungér asked.

“Believe me, Lorenzo’s family has had their fingers in everything for years. They are all connected,” Paulo went on.

“But I am just a… a… pig,” Juanito whispered. “It makes no sense,” Juanito stated.

But like always, Paulo’s knowledge of Lorenzo explained everything to the group.

"My dear Juanito, men like Lorenzo are driven by things we may never understand—things they believe set them apart from the rest," Paulo hissed.

"And what is that?" Juanito asked.

Paulo's tongue flicked in and out of their mouth a few times.

"Pride. And for men like him, nothing is more dangerous," Paulo hissed.

The group stared at Lorenzo in the distant truck, taking in what Paulo surmised.

They started to hurry on their way to get as far away from Lorenzo as possible. But Juanito's large girth slowed him down even though everyone else picked up their pace.

"You must hurry, Juanito," Ungér pleaded.

"You and Paulo, go on ahead; I will distract them." Juanito proceeded to plop down behind a bush to catch his breath. Paulo slithered back toward him.

"Go protect Ungér, I will be fine. Go!" Juanito could only think about Ungér at that moment. But Juanito could not convince Paulo.

"It is not Ungér they are interested in," Paulo stated. Zephyr took charge.

"Ungér, don't stop. There is a cave up ahead. I will meet you there," Zephyr encouraged Ungér as they watched Juanito and Paulo move toward the cocoa farm.

"Don't worry, I will help Juanito and Paulo, somehow," Zephyr yelled over to Ungér. She debated, but only for a minute then took off for the cave as Zephyr flew back to catch up with Juanito and Paulo.

Meanwhile, Juanito huffed and puffed as he arrived at the cocoa tree orchard. Paulo slithered up next to Juanito, surprising him.

"What are you doing staying here with me? You will get caught! Save yourself and help Ungér," Juanito pleaded.

"I am tired of leaving those who need help--" But before Paulo could finish their thought…

SCREEEECH! Lorenzo and the truck pulled up and slammed on the brakes when they saw Juanito in the cocoa orchard. Lorenzo seemed confused.

“There he is! Who put that… that sweater on him?” Lorenzo leaped out of the truck; the chase was on.

Juanito, though tired and worn out, put up quite a fight. He knocked over Lorenzo as he came down one row of the cocoa tree orchard. Paulo slid across another row and Santiago tripped over him. Paulo slithered away so fast, by the time Santiago got back on his feet Paulo was nowhere to be seen.

The cartel driver seemed to have Juanito cornered. He leaped for Juanito and struggled with him in a bear like hug. But then a dark shadow appeared overhead. The driver, confused, looked up as he struggled with Juanito…

PLOP! A large load of condor poop from Zephyr landed right in his face… while the cartel driver wiped it away, Juanito bit his hand.

“Ouch, *cochino*! That hurt,” the driver focused on his injured hand. Juanito made his escape. He lost everyone chasing him and he headed to the farmhouse. He hid behind a large water trough and watched the old farmer who now sat on the porch in a rickety chair.

Lorenzo rushed over and grabbed the local farmer by his shirt.

“Where is that pig? Are you hiding him?” Lorenzo pleaded.

“Are you crazy? Why would I do that?” the farmer countered. “I am the one who called. Catch him! I want my reward!”

Juanito watched it all from behind the water trough. He noticed an enormous rodent that appeared to be pregnant made her way toward the cocoa orchard. She carried very thin twigs, remnants of string, bits of cloths that she gathered to make for her soon to be born rodent pups…

SNAP! All eyes turned to the rodent whose front legs were now stuck in a trap, her nesting material tossed in front of her.

“Santiago, see if that pig went that way!” Lorenzo barked.

Juanito eyed the rodent in the trap and then Lorenzo and his men. The rodent caught Juanito’s eye, and her look was one of desperation. Juanito could not expose himself. *It is just a rodent. Why should I put myself in harm's way for her?* Juanito thought.

As Santiago came closer to the rodent, Juanito seemed to struggle with what to do. He thought of Ungér and how she said we had to help each other... *that's what friends do…* Santiago got closer to the rodent…*But she is not my friend...she is just some rat. Why should I care?* Juanito debated with himself. The rat noticed and pleaded her case to Juanito.

"Hey, chunky cheeks, how about a hand here, or maybe that snout of yours would work? I'm uh, Rita Ratón and I have some uh, pressing matters I need to attend to, if you know what I mean," Rita sarcastically squealed.

But Rita's panic was visible in her eyes. Confliction in Juanito's.

Santiago went up and down the rows around Rita, not noticing her or Juanito behind the nearby trough whispering to Rita.

"I would help you if I could, but it's too dangerous," Juanito whispered.

Rita squirmed in the trap.

"Not as dangerous as it is for me. I was just minding my own business gathering nesting material for my soon arriving rodent pups. I thought that boa constrictor buddy of yours was sizing me up for a mid-week brunch. He scared me and now I am stuck in this thing. Any minute they will toss me in that water trough in front of you and it will be all over, and they'll see you too," Rita pointed out.

Juanito ducked his head as Santiago seemed to look in his direction but then moved on.

Rita was becoming desperate. She knew time was running out.

"Look my blubbery friend, you are being hunted as I am being hunted. That's why this thing so rudely grabbed my legs," Rita explained.

"Find him! Find that pig already," Lorenzo yelled from across the property.

Juanito slinked lower behind the trough as Rita momentarily played dead until the attention went elsewhere. Rita made her last plea to Juanito.

"These humans hunt anything they want and do whatever they want with it. Eat you, snag me in a trap, get rid of us with poisons and pesticides, stuff some other big animals as a trophy to put on a wall. They act like this world is theirs and theirs alone, and we have no place in it except for their fancy. I was put on this earth to be me, to have my babies. I am just being me. So, what do you say, a little help here… please?" Rita begged.

As Lorenzo looked around the property, Juanito noticed that the cartel driver tossed a metal object with a short skinny barrel to Santiago. Juanito had never seen anything like it.

The cartel driver eyed Rita in the trap.

"Finish that rodent off," the driver said.

Santiago looked at the metal object with the short barrel… and then his eyes drifted to Rita… and so did Juanito's. Something about the object bothered Juanito.

Juanito bolted for Rita and used his snout and teeth to free her legs from the trap.

"You're all right porky," Rita smiled.

"Run!" Juanito whispered to her, exposing himself as Rita hurried away.

"There! Catch that pig. He is right there," Lorenzo shouted.

Santiago and the cartel driver jumped on Juanito who put up quite the fight. Zephyr flew overhead and circled closer and closer to the driver and Santiago…

… and dropped another load of poop on the cartel driver's head.

Furious, the driver grabbed the metal object from Santiago and aimed it at Zephyr.

Juanito, wide eyed, knocked over the driver and the metal thing with the barrel went flying into the nearby water trough. As Zephyr flew away, Juanito eyed his friend. He started to waddle away as fast as he could, but then realized he was putting his friends in harm's way by resisting.

Juanito did one of his three hundred-and-sixty-degree waddles. But this was not a dance of joy. He was concerned for his friend Zephyr and that metal barrel thing that was now in the water trough. Juanito's circular motion was to take in all his options. He could not let Zephyr be hurt because of him… Juanito took one last glance at the orchard. Maybe he should make a break for it. *But Zephyr... she'd be defenseless.*

Did they have another metal barrel thing? he thought to himself. His heart pounded… As everyone focused on Zephyr flying overhead, Juanito took a step toward freedom. But then that awful metal barrel thing glinted in the water again. And Zephyr was still right there. Juanito had no way of knowing that the metal barrel thing was harmless in the water. And he did not know if maybe they had another one. So Juanito did something he never would have done before this trip… he gave himself up to Santiago to make sure Zephyr would not get hurt because of him.

"You have wasted enough of my time," Lorenzo yelled at Juanito. "Let us get you back to the salter and be on with this!"

Santiago and the cartel driver struggled to get Juanito into the truck bed.

"By this time tomorrow he will be covered in salt, curing; *my most prize-ham-to be,"* Lorenzo shouted to the sky. He jumped in the truck, slammed on the door, and yelled to the driver.

"Back on the road! To the airport!" he ordered.

Santiago and the driver jumped in the truck too, the old farmer watching them all.

From the window of the truck, Lorenzo tossed some paper money at the feet of the farmer who chased the bills in the wind.

Juanito noticed Rita eyed him from the field as they drove off. She had returned to gathering twigs and leaves to build a nest. She mouthed the words ‘thank you’ to Juanito. They nodded to each other. What Juanito had not realized was that Paulo had slithered his way into the back of the crew cab truck bed when they were on the farm. Their massive size curled up under an old tarp.

“Paulo, what are you doing?” Juanito whispered. Paulo had always slithered away from confrontation. The same way they had slithered away from the Amazon when Juanito and Ungér first met Paulo; they were escaping south, away from the destruction of their habitat. But something about their new-found friendship with Juanito made them throw caution to the wind.

Paulo grinned, their snake body coiling next to Juanito to protect him. “Saving your bacon, my friend. Besides, I've always wanted to see more of Colombia.”

The colorful boa constrictor slowly raised their head to the back window of the crew cab truck. Lorenzo sensed something and turned around. Paulo’s tongue darted in and out of their mouth as they hissed loudly.

“Stop the truck! I do not want that snake hurting my prized pig!” Lorenzo ordered the cartel driver.

The truck screeched to a stop. The truck bed’s doors swung open, revealing Lorenzo's smiling, smug face and his trusted worker, Santiago. Lorenzo eyed Paulo and leaned into Juanito.

“Your little adventure is over, Juanito.” Lorenzo seemed perplexed that Paulo slithered in front of Juanito to protect him. Lorenzo gestured to Santiago, and he reluctantly put an electric prod to Paulo, who moved out of the way. Lorenzo leaned into Juanito and laughed. “Not even your long, slippery friend here can help you.”

Santiago seemed to be embarrassed as he and Juanito locked eyes.

Speaking with courage he did not know he had, Santiago did not hold back and distracted Lorenzo.

"May I ask Don Lorenzo a question? I understand your desire for wealth is why you continue with your family's companies and harvest so much of the lumber in the Amazon." Santiago stared at Don Lorenzo and then back to Juanito. "But why are you so obsessed with making this pig into a prized ham? Why are you chasing him so?"

Lorenzo gave Santiago a dismissive glare; like how dare he ask such a question to his boss. But Santiago's eyes showed no judgement, just curiosity, making it difficult for Don Lorenzo not to answer.

"Before you criticize my business ventures, understand the harvesting of the lumber you speak of is what pays for the very food on your table. So, I would not be so quick to judge if I were you," Don Lorenzo lectured.

Then, something even more surprising... a hint of vulnerability from Don Lorenzo. He climbed into the back of the truck with Santiago, sitting across from Juanito and Paulo. He cracked each one of his knuckles, as if relieving the pent-up stress buried in his fingers would make it easier for him to explain his reasoning to Santiago. Don Lorenzo kept an eye on Paulo, who coiled up to conserve space, but did not move. It was as if Paulo wanted to hear his answer to Santiago's question.

"You want to know why?" Don Lorenzo's voice was low, almost painful. "Because I have to prove him wrong. I was just Lorenzo before I inherited my title of Don,'" he sighed.

Santiago was confused.

"Prove who wrong?" Santiago pressed curiously.

Lorenzo sighed, his usual bravado cracking. "My mother died when she gave birth to me. I always felt like my father blamed me. I had no older brothers and sisters. It was just me. Each day with my father made me wish I had not been born," Lorenzo explained with moist eyes.

Juanito and Paulo listened to every word as Lorenzo continued...

"My father, the other ranchers, and pig farmers; everyone said I would never amount to anything. I was always a runt, barely surviving my birth, you see. Too small and too weak to work the ranch. But I swore I would show them. My father was most proud of his prized ham win; much prouder than he was of being my father."

Lorenzo stared out at nothing, teary-eyed.

"So, I told myself. I would prove him so wrong. I would produce the finest, most expensive ham in the world. And Juanito is my ticket to that dream."

Santiago seemed confused. "Don Lorenzo, is this what you want? Chasing animals across the world, destroying habitats? Is this the legacy you want to leave just to prove a point?"

Lorenzo looked taken aback. "I... I just want to prove I could do something great."

Santiago stepped forward with courage, stating the obvious.

"But Don Lorenzo, if you use inheritance to <u>buy</u> the pig and not raise him yourself, what does that prove?"

But before Lorenzo could respond, the truck lurched forward. The cartel driver, impatient with the delay, had decided to continue their journey.

"Stop, you fool!"

In the chaos of the sudden movement, Paulo saw their chance. With lightning speed, they wrapped themself around Lorenzo's hands and arms, temporarily stopping him. Lorenzo was at first scared, but then mad.

"What are you doing! You... slimy devil snake! Release me!" Lorenzo panicked.

Santiago just watched, not wanting to be a party to either side.

Lorenzo, his hands restrained by Paulo, yelled at the driver to stop again.

"STOP OR I PAY YOU NOTHING!" Lorenzo raged.

As the truck screeched to a halt again and the driver rushed to the back, Paulo released Lorenzo. But not before Juanito jumped from the open tailgate and escaped into the bush. Paulo quickly followed and slithered into the dense Colombian jungle in pursuit of Juanito as Lorenzo argued with the cartel driver.

"What were you thinking?" Don Lorenzo yelled.

Zephyr circled overhead to lead Paulo and Juanito to the cave and Ungér. They hid in the lush bushes for a minute to watch Lorenzo.

Lorenzo, realizing what had happened, pushed Santiago away and shooed him down the road. Juanito and Paulo listened to every word from the cover of the bushes.

The seed of doubt that Santiago had planted about Lorenzo not proving anything with Juanito, bloomed into a fuming tirade. Lorenzo had to blame someone. "Why did I even bring you? It is your fault they got away! You are fired! Leave, you no longer work for me!"

Santiago took the high road. "I just told you the truth, Don Lorenzo. You are pursuing an unearned legacy."

Lorenzo tossed a stone at Santiago, who continued on his way. Santiago eyed the stone and just shook his head. He spotted a truck loaded with workers heading to harvest cocoa beans and coffee; crops that would never involve the slaughter of animals. He smiled, knowing this was his chance for a new beginning.

Santiago reached up and unpinned his worker's badge - the gold 'LVE' of Lorenzo Valdez Enterprises gleaming one last time in the sun before he let it fall to the dusty road.

"Goodbye, Don Lorenzo," he called back. "You can keep your slaughterhouses and logging operations. From now on, I will work only with what continues to grow from the earth."

Santiago flagged down the truck and jumped on the back with the other workers. As the truck pulled away, he breathed deeply, taking in the sweet scent of coffee and cocoa beans and the smell of his new life, one where he would never again have to compromise his love of animals.

Lorenzo raised his fist in anger as the truckload of workers and Santiago rumbled by. "You will see it is not so simple! Whatever land that is cleared for farming affects some animals!" Lorenzo yelled up to Santiago.

"But we can do much better finding a balance, Don Lorenzo, much better," Santiago yelled down to him. The truck of farm workers continued on, but not before Lorenzo chased the truck down the road and yelled out one last parting shot…

“Balance, you say? Progress sometimes must upset the balance with tough choices!” Lorenzo’s words fell on deaf ears, except for Juanito’s and Paulo’s…

They watched the whole exchange and then disappeared deeper into the lush foliage, leaving Lorenzo standing in the dust, more determined than ever to catch them.

Zephyr flapped her wings to lead Juanito and Paulo to Ungér’s cave.

As they went deeper into the jungle, Juanito turned to Paulo. “Do you think that worker got through to him, even a little?”

Paulo shrugged. “Who knows? But at least now we understand him better.”

As they continued their journey to reunite with Ungér and Zephyr, Juanito was moved to moist eyes when they met up with Ungér at the cave.

“I am so glad you are safe, Juanito,” Ungér sighed with equally moist eyes. Ungér obviously was no longer disappointed in Juanito. She was so happy to see him.

Paulo just rolled their eyes.

"Uh, nice to see you too, Ungér," Paulo whined.

"Of course, I am glad to see you Paulo… and Zephyr too," Ungér countered.

But the look between Ungér and Juanito was different. The depth of their friendship was clear.

A crystal-clear stream bubbled up over jagged, colorful reddish-brown rocks as they walked along a sandy, volcanic enriched path. The fertile ground kept Juanito occupied. As they went farther north, the soil became sandier. Juanito's snout followed some scent he could not let go of.

Juanito dug furiously with his hooves, displacing the sandy soil covered with the yellow and orange tinge of decomposed leaves and plants.

"What is it, Juanito?" Ungér wondered.

Juanito smiled as his hooves dug up lots of light brown shells of *Arachis* wild peanuts. The bounty rained down as they scattered side to side of Juanito… He finally stopped as Ungér and even Zephyr partook of them, and then Juanito.

"I told you I would make it up to you; for taking the wrong path and eating all the chuno. My snout close to the ground came in handy, huh?" Juanito proudly spoke. They all laughed, then were on their way again after filling up on the wild peanuts.

But Juanito could not help but wonder if their encounter with Lorenzo might have changed more than just <u>their</u> path…

Chapter 7:
Pitfalls of the Panamanian Jungle

Acorn of wisdom:
The same three plants - corn, beans, and squash - have been grown together by farmers from Mexico through Guatemala, El Salvador, Honduras, Costa Rica, and Panama for over 5,000 years, a tradition that continues today.

The humid air of one of the densest jungles on earth, the *Darién Panamanian Jungle*, made it near impossible for the sweatered Juanito and his friends to make any real progress. Thick vines and *epiphytes*, those plants whose vines grew on other plants, all competed for a glimpse of the sun that was blocked out by huge mahogany and kapok trees. Juanito and the others stopped and huddled in a small clearing. They had been fortunate enough to slip away from the pursuit of Lorenzo during a chaotic river crossing. But the sound of distant shouts told them their rest would be brief.

"This jungle is the thickest I have ever seen. At least they won't be able to use trucks to chase us," bleated Ungér.

"We can't keep running forever," Paulo hissed, their serpentine body now tense. "Sooner or later, Lorenzo will catch up to us again."

Zephyr nodded in agreement, her wings drooping. Juanito looked at each of his companions and saw fatigue and uncertainty in their eyes.

However, to Juanito, the goal stayed the same regardless of the setbacks: The River of Nueces. Juanito knew he had to step up. Not just for him, but for his journey mates.

Standing tall, Juanito addressed his friends with a passion that surprised even himself.

"My friends, I know we're all tired. I know we are scared. This is our journey, our quest. But if you are spent. I will stop. This is not just about me. It is about us. I will do whatever you all want."

Was this the same Juanito, who wouldn't share a single acorn with a baby pig? The same Juanito who never worried about anyone but himself?

Juanito was changing. Even if he wavered from time to time…

He was inspired.

Zephyr, Paulo and Ungér lowered their eyes.

Paulo raised a skeptical eye and verbalized what they were all thinking. What they were hesitant to share with the hopeful Juanito.

"But Juanito... this place... this River of Nueces… it... it could just be a myth." Juanito eyed the doubtful three. They fidgeted with their uncertainty. Juanito took a minute to gather himself but then spoke.

"Maybe it is a myth. Maybe it doesn't exist." Juanito conceded. "But what if it is not a myth? What if there is a place where we can all be safe and be ourselves?"

Juanito moved over to a shady spot under a giant tropical *Ceiba* tree that was common to the Darién jungle. He was just as tired as the others and the heaviness of his body was more evident than the heaviness in his heart. Was this just a folly? Was he just wasting everyone's time? Their eyes were focused on him. Juanito waddled back over to the three of them.

Paulo slithered up on top of a boulder to look down at them all. It was difficult to tell if there was determination in Paulo's eyes or were they having second thoughts about this journey? Zephyr flapped her wings and flew up and sat next to Paulo.

Juanito and Ungér stood alone in the clearing. Juanito looked back at where they had come from and then at the powerful thick jungle in front of them. He lowered his head and snout below Ungér's face. He lifted her chin up with his snout to look in her eyes.

"Ungér, my dear friend. You have wandered for so long, never having a place to call home. What if The River of Nueces could be that home? A place where your fleece can grow as it wishes. Where nature regulates its length, not humans; or not fear you will be turned into mutton. Maybe there is such a place where you can rest and no longer wander, without worrying about the next journey?"

Ungér's eyes glistened with unshed tears. "Oh, Juanito, do you think it <u>really</u> exists?"

Juanito nuzzled her. "I have to believe it does. For all of us."

He looked up at Zephyr, perched right next to Paulo on the boulder. Zephyr seemed to perk up, flapping her wings. Juanito eyed Paulo, who uncoiled slightly with a glimmer of hope in their eyes… Paulo then proceeded to slither down off the boulder and coil next to Juanito.

Juanito stamped one of his cloven hooves for emphasis. "I say we keep going. Until there is no more running, no more hiding. We make for The River of Nueces and face whatever comes together. What do you say?"

The distant calls of jungle birds broke a moment of silence…

Then, one by one, his friends nodded…

"I'm still with you, Juanito," Ungér said. "Wherever this journey leads."

"Count me in," Zephyr declared. "I'll be your eyes in the sky."

Paulo uncoiled. "Well, someone has to keep you all out of trouble. I am in."

Just as they were about to set off, a crashing sound came from the nearby undergrowth. All alone and distraught, Lorenzo burst into the clearing, his face red with exertion and rage.

All that had happened to him seemed to make him more stubborn, more driven. From catcalls in the streets of Buenos Aires when he introduced Juanito, to the pointed words from Santiago, nothing changed him. His warped view of redemption was the only view that mattered to him.

"There you are... you troublesome *prized ham-to-be*!" he yelled. "It will be satisfying to show you off to the world and show everyone how wrong my father was about me!"

Juanito and the animals usually never spoke above a whisper in front of humans unless they were kindred spirits like Chaska. But Juanito eyed his *compadres* and shocked them when he spoke and offered a verbal olive branch to Lorenzo.

"It is never too late to change. To find your path. Make your <u>own</u> destiny Don Lorenzo." Juanito spoke peacefully.

Lorenzo, though the look on his face hearing Juanito speak was one of extreme confusion, he could not fathom the depth of the truth Juanito laid in front of him. A different path that would fill the hole in his heart, a hole he blamed on his father and others. Lorenzo did not want to accept that his jealousy was his motivation… that he truly had been wronged and holding Juanito's hindquarters over his head in the ham festival would prove to him, his deceased father, and the entire world that he was someone; someone his father was wrong about…

He lashed out at Juanito as if he was the mythical Argentinian fabled werewolf monster.

"You know nothing of what you speak, you evil beast... you... you *Lobizón!"*

Paulo slithered forward and pushed Juanito aside. He was face to face with the one who had destroyed his habitat. He serpentined back and forth trying to muster the courage to speak to Lorenzo… but it was not easy to do.

Lorenzo's boots sank deeper into the quicksand, his panic giving way to a grim realization what his fate might be. He slowed his struggle and his breath became heavy. The weight of his choices pressed down on him. The thick vines and towering ceiba trees stood like giant witnesses to his fate.

Paulo finally coiled near the edge of the quicksand and lifted their shimmering head and spoke to Lorenzo with a confident voice.

"You hunted us across an entire continent, tore through our lands with greed, and now the jungle reclaims you," Paulo hissed. Their golden eyes locked onto Lorenzo's. "You wanted to prove yourself worthy of your father's name? Tell me, Don Lorenzo, did you ever stop to ask if you were worthy of the very land you trampled beneath your boots? The very land your father trampled upon before you."

Lorenzo's lips parted, but no words came. He had spent a lifetime convincing himself that his conquest over his father's achievements would be his legacy and that he was the one betrayed, the one harmed by his father's actions. But in that moment… when the jungle had taken back control of whose legacy would survive… he felt something foreign.

He lowered his head as he slowly sank deeper into the light brown milky pit. Juanito and Ungér exchanged looks of surprise with Zephyr. Paulo coiled up a bit taller. As he looked down on Lorenzo, he seemed a bit confused. The mighty Lorenzo seemed timid… The not so motley crew all thought the same thing at once as they stared at Lorenzo… Lorenzo was…

… ashamed…

"My father…" he muttered, his voice barely more than a rasp. "He said I was nothing. That I was too small. Too weak. I thought if I achieved something greater than him, I could bury any doubt that I had… that I was worth something. That my mother did not die in vain!" he sobbed.

Ungér, moved by Lorenzo's words, stepped forward.

"Don Lorenzo… we are <u>all</u> worth something," she stated. She eyed her journey mates one by one and then took a step closer to Lorenzo…

"We are all… enough," Ungér insisted.

Silence seem to come over the jungle. As if the very birds and animals Lorenzo and his family's actions before him had harmed, wanted to hear what Lorenzo had to say.

But surprisingly, Paulo was not finished.

"And with your actions, you destroyed any enduring legacy," Paulo countered. "And for what? A fortune built on ruins? To pound your chest for some empty achievement that no one cares about? Your legacy will be carved into the corpses of trees and creatures who will never see another sunrise. And for what? To raise Juanito's cured hindquarters above your head one day? To prove something to your father who is no longer here? And really wasn't even here for you when he was alive!"

"Paulo, enough!" Ungér insisted.

"Yes, enough, Paulo," Juanito agreed.

The vines trembled in the humid breeze. The birds of the canopy—those who had once fled from the howling chainsaws of Lorenzo's men—now watched in silence.

"I know now it was wrong," Lorenzo whispered, his voice catching. The fight had left his body. He no longer struggled. "I was wrong to be so blind, so driven."

Paulo's coils tightened against the roots of an ancient kapok tree, their heart racing. For so long, they had wanted this moment. To watch Lorenzo crumble. To hear him admit to his sins.

… But now that it was here, Paulo felt something else… Paulo hissed and moved their head back and forth. Paulo was definitely struggling with it all. Paulo eyed Lorenzo sinking away and then their journey mates. Their hesitation was replaced with…

… A desperate, aching need to save Lorenzo.

"Grab on to me," Paulo urged, stretching their long, muscular body across the pit. Paulo wrapped their tail around the base of a nearby tree to secure themselves to rescue Lorenzo out of the slimy quicksand.

"Hold on. I can pull you free," Paulo urged Lorenzo.

Lorenzo's fingers brushed against the smooth scales. He almost took the offer. Almost. But then, he smiled—softly, sincerely—for what might have been the first time in his life.

"No," he said, voice gentle. "This is my reckoning."

Paulo's coils trembled with frustration. "Don't be a fool! Like Juanito said. You could change. You—"

But Lorenzo only shook his head. "You change. Take what you know. Do something with it. Save what I destroyed." He exhaled sharply, shoulders sinking. "If you try to save me, you'll only sink too."

A beat of silence. A long, painful moment.

… And then, Lorenzo let go…

Paulo recoiled, hissing in anguish as the earth swallowed Lorenzo whole.

Juanito and the others stood frozen, watching as the last ripples of quicksand settled, erasing any trace of the man who had once pursued them so relentlessly. The jungle, indifferent to his fall, resumed its quiet symphony of chirping cicadas and rustling leaves.

For a long time, Paulo didn't move. Their eyes were fixed on the empty space where Lorenzo had been. And then, something within them shifted.

In that moment, Juanito felt an unexpected wave of sadness for the man who had chased them so far. Ungér stepped closer, pressing her muzzle gently against Juanito.

"This isn't the way I thought this journey would go," she quietly stated to Juanito.

Juanito didn't answer right away. His eyes lingered on the spot where Lorenzo had disappeared in the quicksand.

Finally, he exhaled…

… "Me neither."

The rainforest grew quiet again, but then the soft sounds of jungle birds cackling and cooing broke the silence.

Ungér pushed Juanito's snout around, so they were eye to eye. "He was lost, Juanito," Ungér muttered. "Just like we all are, in our own way. Maybe it was too late for him… but it is not too late for us."

A strange feeling came over them all. For so long they had been trying to avoid Lorenzo and now he was gone, just like that; what they perceived to be their biggest obstacle. The one person that represented so much grief for them was no longer a threat.

The silence let them all process what had happened. But Paulo was having a challenging time understanding everything that had just transpired.

"What is it, Paulo?" Ungér asked.

“I’m not sure. But I feel now that he is gone, maybe I can help.”

“Help with what?” Zephyr tilted her head.

“We must keep going, to find a way of living with nature, not against it,” Juanito stated.

But Paulo was not so sure. They slithered back and forth. They seemed to be reviewing everything they went through; how they had come to this particular point at this particular time.

“No, Lorenzo was right I must do what he said,” Paulo nodded their head.

“Uh, exactly what did he say?” questioned Zephyr.

“Save what he destroyed,” Paulo hissed.

Paulo slithered back and forth. They were energized like they had an epiphany. As if something became so clear to them about what they must do.

“I joined you all because I thought it was hopeless; that nothing could be done to restore my home. But Lorenzo Valdez is right. I may be able to change things.”

Juanito studied Paulo. He could see in their eyes they were different, focused.

“I must go back.” They were all shocked to see Paulo slither away.

And then, something extraordinary happened. Paulo's scales began to shimmer in a way none of them had ever seen before. Though it usually took weeks for a boa to shed their skin, Paulo's transformation seemed as sudden as their change of heart. In moments, their old skin fell away, revealing brilliant new, glimmering scales underneath that dazzled in the sunlight.

“Are you going where I think you are? Didn't you say that you were rejected by others down there? You couldn't be who you knew in your heart you were?” Juanito asked.

Paulo glanced back at their shed skin lying in the grass like a ghost of their former self, then faced their friends with renewed determination in their eyes.

“Yes, that is true. But if I return to the Amazon, I can let everyone know that there is hope. That even in his dying moments, Lorenzo wanted change. That I should lead that change. I can inspire others to plant new trees and reforest and not only help repair my habitat. Maybe help others to be more accepting of others like me too."

… Paulo's powerful words hung in the air…

Zephyr landed next to Paulo and cocked her head.

"You really think you will make a difference?" she squealed.

"I... need to try..." Paulo stated in a determined voice.

"But we have come so far… I believe… we are so close." Juanito pleaded.

Paulo smiled at Ungér. "Sometimes, the longest way around is the shortest way home."

Ungér smiled back in agreement. Paulo eyed each one of them.

"I must show others what I have learned from you." Paulo eyed the path south. The path Paulo thought they must now take… Paulo could tell the others were still confused.

"You all are looking for a place to call home. I had a home in the Amazon. Besides, I doubt I would survive in the drier climate where you are headed anyway," Paulo said, downplaying their noble gesture.

Juanito's internal battle with selfishness rose to the surface again. "But I don't understand? We need you-" Juanito interjected.

"Stop, Juanito, Stop!" All eyes turned to Ungér. Her stare let them all know she understood what Paulo must do. Paulo nodded to her in appreciation.

"As long as Lorenzo Valdez was in my world, I knew there was no chance that my home would survive. Now trees can be replanted; the rivers undammed, and maybe even stop the strip mining scarring the land," Paulo went on.

Juanito listened closely to try and understand Paulo's vision. Paulo summed it all up in one powerful sentence what their new mission would be:

"We must figure out a way to live together, humans and animals alike. To take care of each other and our mother earth."

"We are all better for knowing you Paulo," Ungér chimed in.

Ungér, Juanito and Zephyr watched Paulo slowly slither away. Their eyes followed them until Paulo was no longer in sight. Juanito broke the silence with a truthful observation:

“For Paulo, the bravest thing isn't moving on to a new life… it's going back and trying to make things better in their old life.”

Juanito, Ungér and Zephyr, turned and kept heading north. The jungle in front of them proved to be a difficult foe. The next few weeks turned into a month or more; scavenging for food became their biggest obstacle. But Zephyr came through repeatedly, spotting potential bounty from above.

Zephyr, who much like Paulo, seemed to never eat any of the fruits or vegetables they came across, would disappear from time to time but then return…

“Where do you think Zephyr goes when we can’t see her?” Juanito asked.

Again, the wise and worldly Ungér responded the same way as when Juanito inquired of Paulo’s dining habits.

“Believe me, Juanito. You don’t want to know,” Ungér assured him.

Ungér could chew on almost anything for food. But Juanito needed a lot more. Corn harvests and fields of other vegetables and fruits got him by. Strawberries were his favorite. They were all weary and each step seemed more difficult than the last.

They made their way through many more exotic places including *Costa Rica* and their beautiful beaches. Watching Juanito waddle to the water's edge and then try to waddle away from it before the wave got to him made Ungér laugh. Zephyr flew over the deserted beaches and kept a watchful eye out for any danger… today there was none… just a wonderful place to relax and enjoy the sun and ocean breeze. White faced *capuchin* monkeys swung from tree to tree and then hopped on the lush green palm and almond trees that framed the beaches that Juanito and Ungér played on…

The sand on the beach at *Playa Negra* was like nothing any of them had ever seen. A blanket of black, volcanic sand covered the coastline and stretched beyond sight. The crystal blue ocean water that crashed upon the smooth beach, bubbled up into a pinkish, and snow-white foam that lingered on the midnight-colored sands before it dissipated into the air. Seagulls made their way over to check out the strangers but soon noticed Zephyr circling overhead. They quickly flew off in another direction cackling as seagulls do. Ungér smiled at Zephyr and yelled at her.

"You scared them all away, Zephyr," Ungér laughed.

Zephyr circled lower over her and Juanito. "You two can thank me later for not letting them poop on your head," Zephyr cackled.

They could not be happier at the moment; they needed this.

Juanito, still with his thick sweater on, raced to the water's edge again. He did one of his three hundred and sixty degree turns…

"I AM KING OF THE BEACH!" Juanito yelled…

WHACK!

A huge wave knocked Juanito over and he spun around like a top in the volcanic sand and the pink and white sea foam.

"All hail King Juanito of the Waves!" Ungér kidded him.

As quickly as Juanito stood, another wave came.

WHACK!

"Help!" Juanito squealed dramatically, rolling in the foam like a snow angel without wings. "I am being attacked by the ocean!" he giggled.

"You were ruler of absolutely nothing for exactly three seconds!" Ungér roared with laughter.

Zephyr cackled with amusement too. Even the capuchin monkeys watching laughed at Juanito; in fact, the whole jungle seemed to cackle with laughter mimicking Juanito.

This made Ungér laugh even harder.

"The mighty Juanito, conquered by a wave!"

Juanito managed to right himself, his sweater now dotted with wet volcanic sand. He stumbled as he got up because of the weight of the soaked sweater.

"I meant to do that," he said as he steadied himself. He moved closer to Ungér.

"No! No! Don't you dare, Juanito!" Ungér laughed.

Juanito proceeded to shake like a dog spraying Ungér with the ocean and volcanic sand mix. She shook right back at him to shed the sand he had just sprayed upon her.

"I have conquered the ocean," he proudly stated. But then he leaped out of the way of another incoming wave.

They were having so much fun until Zephyr cackled a warning from above nodding over toward the jungle.

Ungér and Juanito at once took notice… they froze in place.

Like always on this journey, danger was close…

A sleek tan and gold skin jaguar eyed them through the tree line. The jaguar, much smaller than the black one with her cubs they saw earlier in the journey, was still a formidable foe… but the jaguar seemed spooked by all the monkeys laughing and slinked away…

The threesome looked around at the beach and realized it was time to go… back on their journey. As Juanito would always say: *The River of Nueces awaits us!*

They gathered together. Juanito and Ungér eyed Zephyr in the sky. She swooped down to let them know what was ahead.

"Next stop… *Nicaragua*," she cackled.

Nicaragua was mostly uneventful. The country was covered with sky blue lakes and majestic volcanoes that soared into the bright white clouds. They managed to sneak rides on some rickety water ferries and even some old horses and buggies that carried feed and supplies to remote villages.

They were amazed as they came across the *Somotos Canyon.* It had spectacular views and rock formations. Waterfalls dotted the *Coco River* as it made its way through ancient, rugged stone walls of orange, beige and gray tones. Its water shimmered with hues of emerald and turquoise under bright sunlight.

Juanito was lucky enough to come across a toppled trash can near a local vendor's food cart. There were some half-eaten, discarded local delicacies. Juanito gorged on the remnants of *nacatamales*: vegetable and beef corn cakes. He even let Ungér have some of the bounty he found… but only after he had his fill, of course.

They made their way out of Nicaragua without coming across many different animals. They were able to pick up their pace because of it.

"I have heard of a place called *El Salvador* that is near here, but I think if we go through *Honduras*, it will be shorter," Ungér explained.

"Shorter is better. So, you do know where this place called Texas is?" Juanito asked.

“No, but my wandering sheep compass knows if it is north, then it will be faster to go through Honduras,” Ungér assured him.

Zephyr agreed from above. “Trust her Juanito, my instincts tell me the same,” she cackled.

All was going well, and they picked up their pace even more as they made their way through Honduras. As they came close to the Honduran and *Guatemala* border, they came across a place called the *Copán* ruins. They were ancient pyramids. The unique multi-stepped structures made them stop and gaze in awe. Juanito craned his neck up at the steep stairs that went all the way up to a ceremonial deck.

“I could never make it up all those stairs,” Juanito marveled. As they hurried through the ruins, many human tourists showed up on buses. The three of them hurried away and came across a large valley…

…. filled with sheep…

Ungér stopped dead in her tracks, teary-eyed.

“My… kind,” was all she could say. Ungér jumped for joy. Her front two hooves bounced up and down on the ground. She did a three-hundred-and-sixty-degree waddle just as Juanito would. A flock! She found a flock! In a beautiful, lush valley.

While Zephyr flew overhead, Juanito felt like he was punched in his oversized gut. *'Ungér's kind'* is all he could think. Sheep spanned endlessly throughout the fertile valley. Juanito feigned happiness for her, but inside he was dying.

"Uh, I am happy for you, Ungér. This is what you always wanted, a new flock," he stated. "Go to them." Juanito turned away so Ungér could not see the tears in his eyes.

Yes! This is everything she wanted! How could she be so lucky? But then her eyes studied Juanito, the ground and the flock.

… She was so… conflicted.

Her eyes caught those in Juanito's disappointed face. He tried to hide his emotions, but Ungér could tell how he felt. She spoke, not sure if she was talking to herself or Juanito.

"I can't leave, not just like that." Juanito seemed confused at her words. This was all so fast, so sudden; a few days earlier she was laughing at Juanito making wingless snow angels in ocean foam on black volcanic beach sand…

… and now he was telling her to leave? But of course, this was her dream… a new flock. Confusion and excitement was visible in her face. She wavered back and forth in her mind. She took a step forward towards the flock but then…

… Ungér hesitated…

She wanted to leap in the fields with all the other sheep, but something made her stand her ground. She had been through so much and become so close to Juanito. How could friendship be so painful? This was not right. It did not feel right in her heart. But as all the other sheep gathered around her, she knew this was her destiny. At some point she was going to have to leave Juanito behind and have a family.

… That could not happen with Juanito…

But why did it hurt so much? Why could he still not be in her life? Ungér looked over at a ram and his sheep partner and their two little offspring next to them. The ram nuzzled with the sheep who nuzzled back. Their two little lamb children moved closer to them as they all eyed Ungér.

A couple of young rams butted heads as a display of interest in Ungér. A traditional battle that male sheep did to impress female sheep of their worthiness.

Juanito moved forward as if to join the battle to show his worth but quickly caught himself. What could he prove that would make any difference?

... *I am not a ram*, he thought.

Ungér tearfully eyed Juanito, who was trying to be strong. *This is what Ungér dreamed of. I must be happy she has found her dream*, Juanito tried to tell himself.

The flock surrounded Ungér to help usher her away, but she could not take her moist eyes off of Juanito.

In that moment she realized how close they'd become to each other. The awkwardness was broken by Zephyr, who swooped down. She eyed Juanito and then Ungér, then stared at the large flock of sheep as they led Ungér away.

"Hey, this is a happy time. Ungér will be with her kind. She can start a family the way she wanted! Hooray for Ungér!" Zephyr tried to change the mood.

Juanito, sucked in a deep breath. The selfish Iberian pig who only cared about himself surprised Ungér. He pushed through the flock and went up to Ungér and nuzzled up against her.

“Just as Conejo was my friend and I had to leave him, I know I must leave you.” Juanito struggled to get the words out. He looked out at the huge flock that filled the lush, green valley.

Ungér remained… hesitant. But in front of her stood everything she wanted: Family, the chance to have lamb offspring, and a beautiful, fertile valley with abundant grasses and thick-leaved plants for her to forage on. She kept trying to tell herself: *You made it Ungér.*

But everything they had been through, all the trials and tribulations, kept bubbling to the surface over and over for her. This journey was so much more than what she wanted. Juanito’s growth shined through. He turned to leave with Zephyr and nodded.

“When one of us is happy. We are all happy. I am happy for you, Ungér. Go, go with them, and know you will always be with me in spirit,” Juanito struggled to say.

Juanito quickly had to waddle away so Ungér would not see his tears. Ungér was so torn between the flock and Juanito’s journey.

She hurried back over in front of him.

"Maybe you can stay here! I am sure it will be okay," Ungér pleaded.

Juanito noticed a cattle ranch and pigs in a pen in the distance. No, he could not stay there. It would be just a matter of time before he was led to his demise. Before he heard about The River of Nueces maybe he would have stayed. After all, *a-ham-to-be* was his destiny in time and he knew it. But the thought of a place where he would not be turned into a ham and just coexist with other animals was now his dream. As much as he would miss Ungér, he knew he had to leave.

The other sheep pushed their way up to Ungér and tried to lead her away. Juanito and Zephyr hurried off. Zephyr flew back and landed next to Ungér which scattered the other bleating sheep. Zephyr opened those huge condor wings and hugged Ungér.

"Don't you worry about Juanito, he will be fine," she cackled.

As Zephyr flew away and caught up with Juanito in the distance, Ungér could not take her eyes off Juanito and tearfully whispered to herself.

"It is not him who I am worried about…"

The other sheep escorted her down the hill toward the huge waiting flock, but she couldn't keep trying to get a glimpse of Juanito…

… but he was gone.

As the journey continued, Juanito sulked.

Juanito and Zephyr plowed forward. The one constant they noticed was that local farmers and ranchers were displaced by large commercial farms. But what concerned Zephyr the most was Juanito. As they left Honduras, Zephyr noticed Juanito always kept looking back.

"She is where she should be Juanito," Zephyr said.

"I know that. I am just, uh, making sure nothing is following us," Juanito countered.

Zephyr landed in front of Juanito, stopping him from going any farther. She tried to encourage Juanito, to try and cheer him up.

"I know it may not be my place, but I was impressed how you managed that back there," Zephyr nodded.

"Managed what?" Juanito uttered.

“You two were close, I know. To escape from a slaughterhouse is not easy. To make it through everything you two did together is something very few could do. ‘Proud’ is a word that comes to mind when I think about knowing you, Juanito,” Zephyr nodded.

“Thanks, Zephyr, it’s just that I never cared about anything but myself before. And I do care about you, Paulo and even my old friend, Conejo,” Juanito began.

“But…?” Zephyr leaned in.

“I don’t know. We just went through so much together and she taught me so much and now she is gone… it is just… hard,” Juanito complained.

“She is not gone Juanito if you keep her memory in your heart,” Zephyr comforted him. “You miss her because she made you better. Made you think about others besides yourself.”

Juanito studied Zephyr. There was something to what she said. He smiled and picked up his pace. Yes, maybe Ungér was still with him… even if it was just in his heart.

The journey bogged down in Guatemala. Train rides and sneaking onto the back of trucks became less of a possibility.

So, they went terribly slow. It seemed like they were making little progress. They made their way into *Antigua*, an Old Spanish Colonial city. Tourist signs showed men in armor and bronze placards that referenced the word *Conquistadors* several times… Juanito seemed to be dragging his hooves. His pace was turtle-like. It was beginning to become evident that Juanito was running out of motivation.

"Enough Juanito! Stay here if you want. But this is not what I signed up for. The River of Nueces, remember?"

Juanito just moped over to a large *Guatemalan Fir* shade tree. He plopped down on the ground, totally spent. "Go on without me. I am too tired; maybe I should just stay here and let them fatten me back up and turn me into ham already."

Zephyr got up in Juanito's face. "Stop feeling sorry for yourself. We are in Guatemala. They don't eat much ham. They will turn you into *carneada* right away and serve you at Sunday dinner."

Juanito got up and started walking again. "Fine, but I want to stop for the day soon. I am tired."

Zephyr just shook her head. “There is a clearing over there behind that old Spanish building. There are some fruit trees over there too.”

Juanito made his way over to the clearing. Zephyr noticed Juanito did not even touch the fallen fruit. She swooped down, deliberately knocking a perfectly ripe mango onto his snout.

“Hey!” Juanito protested.

“Sorry,” Zephyr said, not sorry at all. “My wing must be tired from carrying all this optimism by myself.” She knocked down another mango. It hit Juanito on the head.

“Stop it already, Zephyr. That’s not nice,” Juanito fired back. Zephyr landed next to Juanito.

“What is not nice is for you to be moping like you lost your best friend,” Zephyr told him.

As soon as Zephyr said it, she knew it was the wrong thing to say and knew the response that was coming.

“I did.”

"Things change, Juanito. Things end. That is life. It is how we respond to things that is important." Zephyr waited for a response… there was none.

"Do you think I am here, so many kilometers away from my home in the Andes because I want to be?" Zephyr asked.

Juanito raised his eyes to her, confused. Zephyr moved closer to Juanito.

"I am here because you are my friend, too. I believed in you Juanito. But right now, I'm thinking maybe I made a mistake," she verbally throttled him.

"Because I don't think you believe in yourself anymore."

Juanito just turned away, pensive. Zephyr flew up to the top of the Spanish building, landed, and just stared out. She had said her piece…

A beautiful sunset bounced off the faded adobe covered bricks of the Spanish building and started to disappear behind the orchards. Zephyr sighed as she looked down at a dejected Juanito.

Should I stay with Juanito? Or maybe I should just leave him and find The River of Nueces by myself, she thought.

Zephyr continued to eye Juanito. She had to reconsider her plans if Juanito had given up. Juanito looked up at her and wondered if she would be there in the morning.

As he fell asleep Juanito smiled at the memory of meeting Ungér. How excited they were to become friends even though they were both doomed. But something about their friendship turned their lives around and gave them hope. But Ungér was gone. Juanito realized she was a major part of his motivation to find The River of Nueces. He had pretty much accepted his fate as *a prized-ham-to-be*. But meeting Ungér had changed his life and made him such a better pig. More caring, more motivated to help others… but now he was slipping back to the selfish Juanito. He realized he made Ungér better by being adventurous just as she had made him better… *that's what friends do, Juanito*…he could hear her voice in his head… but yes, he had to accept… she was gone.

Zephyr watched Juanito down below and turned her head. She would not fly off by herself in search of The River of Nueces just yet. She would wait till morning and give Juanito one more chance.

As Zephyr perched, her eyes became weary. *Because we are friends Juanito, and that is what friends do…* Ungér's words that she repeated several times after Zephyr had joined them, were the last thing she remembered before she fell asleep… yes, Ungér had a profound effect on both of them.

The sunrise in the east woke Zephyr up in the morning. The yellow bananas and pinkish hue of the mango skins on the trees caught her attention. She noticed Juanito was still sleeping in the clearing… She also noticed rustling in the thick jungle like bushes just outside the orchard near where Juanito was sleeping.

"Juanito," she cackled. He kept sleeping, his oinks of snoring the only sound. But then the rustling in the bushes became louder, closer.

"Juanito! Wakeup, Juanito!"

Juanito would not wake up. He was done. He rolled over and ignored Zephyr.

"JUANITO WAKE UP!" Zephyr insisted. Juanito turned to her and yelled. "I am done, Zephyr, leave without me!"

Zephyr was so mad, she swooped down next to Juanito. She puffed out her chest and fluffed her wings. She sighed and remembered what she learned from Ungér. And then…

as if she had no choice, profound words of friendship escaped her beak.

“Ungér would not leave you if she was here…”

“… and neither will I…”

The words hit Juanito hard, real hard. He sobbed.

“I am sorry Zephyr you have come all this way for nothing.” Juanito whined.

“On the contrary, Juanito, I have learned so much from you and Ungér,” Zephyr uttered. Zephyr flapped her wings to make Juanito pay attention. He started to speak…

“I just, I just-”

“-Quiet, Juanito, quiet,” Zephyr cut him off…

The crackling in the jungle moved closer.

Zephyr began to panic as the rustling made its way all the way to the edge of the orchard.

“I think it may be a jaguar looking for breakfast,” Zephyr whispered.

The rustling in the bushes became louder and closer.

… Zephyr was in full panic mode.

"RUN, JUANITO, RUN!" Zephyr cackled loudly. "I'LL DO MY BEST TO GIVE YOU TIME, RUN!"

Juanito, totally confused, stumbled off, away from the rustling noise. Zephyr spread her huge wings as if to make herself bigger in the eyes of the anticipated predator.

Juanito tripped over a dead tree branch and rolled over. He peeked back at Zephyr in anticipation of watching her meet her fate. Juanito closed his eyes as something came out of the bushes.

… It was… Ungér!

"Ungér!" Zephyr's voice made Juanito open his eyes. There in the clearing now stood Ungér. Juanito shook his head. *Am I dreaming? How can this be?*

No, he wasn't dreaming; it truly was Ungér!

Juanito waddled over to her as fast as he could, stumbling on another tree branch. Zephyr, enveloped Ungér with her wings in a hug, but quickly stepped aside as Juanito came barreling over. He could not slow himself down enough and knocked Ungér over in his excitement.

Ungér chuckled and got back on her feet.

"Uh, I was going to ask if you missed me, but I think you just answered that," she smiled.

The three friends nudged each other with affection. Much like old friends who haven't seen each other in a long time.

"Come on you guys, I haven't been gone that long," Ungér laughed.

Juanito did one of his three-hundred-and-sixty-degree waddle turns in front of her.

"But I never, uh, we never expected to see you again. You had everything you wanted there. Why did you leave? You did leave, didn't you? Or is this just a visit? How did you find us? Zephyr thought you were a jaguar- "

"Juanito! Catch your breath. One question at a time, please," she smiled.

A tourist bus pulled up in the distance and humans started to get off. Ungér noticed and ushered her friends away from the ancient Spanish ruins…

"We better get going," Ungér proclaimed confidently.

"Go where?" Juanito eyed her with hopeful eyes.

"North," is all she said.

She took off heading north with Zephyr and Juanito staring at each other. This was all so unexpected. Ungér was back with them. Zephyr took flight and circled above as she always did. Juanito watched his friends continue the journey to The River of Nueces. He sighed deeply with a cautious happiness as they indeed headed…

… North...

Juanito watched Ungér on the path in front of him. He had so many questions he wanted to ask her. But he didn't ask a single one. No, he thought it might change her mind, and she would go back to the flock she just left. Ungér seemed to be deep in thought on the path as jungle bushes brushed up against her, so Juanito just left her alone. Zephyr dived-bombed them from time-to-time to make sure they were okay… they were.

The mood on the journey was different and Juanito and Ungér were cordial and obviously happy to be with each other again. But it was as if something was being left unsaid. Juanito did not pry anymore about why Ungér had returned to being with them on their journey. There was a certain determination in Ungér. Juanito decided he would wait till she wanted to talk about it and not bother her until she was ready. Ungér would smile at him from time to time with a deeper smile than before. He was so happy his friend was back with them… but he hoped it was for the right reasons. Hopefully, nothing bad happened that she had to run from… He would find out another day.

But now he would just enjoy her company again.

After taking a wrong turn as they came out of Guatemala toward the *Yucatan Peninsula*, Zephyr flying overhead, noticed right away and got them turned around and they headed north into...

… *Mexico...*

Chapter 8:
From Cobblestones to Desert Sands

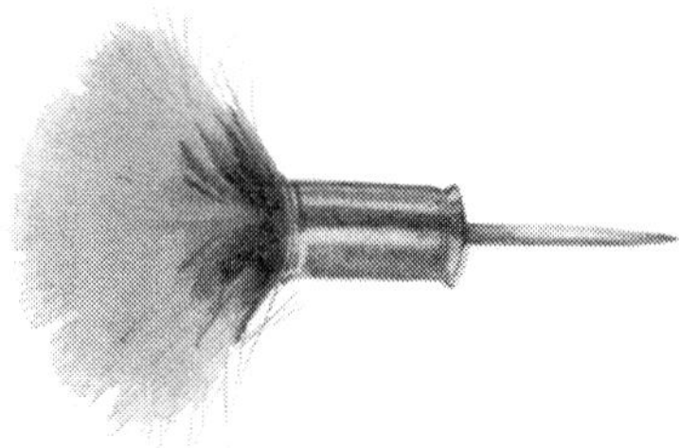

Acorn of wisdom:

From ancient cobblestone towns to busy cities and vast deserts, Mexico has many of Earth's landscapes in a single country.

The River of Nueces still loomed as a promise of hope and acceptance on the horizon. But as Juanito led his friends northward, he could not shake the feeling that their most significant challenges were still in front of them.

The trek through Mexico seemed like it took forever…

In the colonial city of *Oaxaca,* they crept along ancient cobblestone streets between buildings painted in bright yellows and blues, past churches with massive wooden doors, and through plazas where the scent of fresh tortillas and chocolate filled the air.

"That smells so good," Juanito whiffed. "I am so hungry."

"Not again, Juanito. You just ate those peppers," Ungér insisted.

Juanito, embarrassed, scraped the ground with his hoof.

"I think that is why I am hungry again. They were spicy and went right through me," Juanito smiled.

"Too much information," Zephyr cackled from above.

Juanito could always find something to eat, somewhere. A few discarded tortillas here, a few bites of chocolate there. Juanito scored again but hesitated after tasting the chocolate.

"It tastes good… but something tells me I may regret it," Juanito frowned.

"Go with your gut, Juanito," Ungér chuckled.

"Very funny," Juanito replied. He sniffed the broken pieces of chocolate and moved on. Juanito was rather good about staying away from foods that didn't agree with him.

They continued northward past vast fields of blue *agave* plants stretching to the horizon, and through dense jungles where more howler monkeys squealed in the canopy above.

As they made their way north to *Mexico City*, they passed by two incredible volcanoes; one of them, *Popocatépetl*, spilled some ash like smoke into the sky out of its snow crowned peak. It was as if the ash was competing with the fluffy white clouds in the surrounding blue sky. While it wasn't an eruption or anything for them to worry about, it did make Juanito hurry up a bit.

"Keep moving Juanito," Zephyr yelled down from the sky. "You don't want to become toasted *carnitas* would you?" Zephyr joked…

Nevertheless, they did pick up their pace.

The three of them finally entered Mexico City and it overwhelmed them. They discovered what seemed like an endless stream of produce trucks heading to the city's massive food market. They came upon one of the trucks that had a flat tire. The loading plank was in place as the driver rolled a spare tire down it. As he started to fix the flat, Juanito and Ungér waddled up the plank, unseen. Their faces lit up at the sight of corn and squash, the driver none the wiser as they hid among the vegetables. All the while, Zephyr kept an eye on Juanito and Ungér from above.

The driver finally fixed the flat, tossed the flat tire in the back, put up the plank and drove off… Juanito and Ungér got up from their hiding spot and moved up to the rear gate and looked out. They became wide-eyed as they drove through the heart of the sprawling city.

The truck wound its way through the maze of streets, past towering buildings until they finally emerged on the city's northern outskirts. The terrain changed dramatically as they went.

One day they would be trudging through humid valleys filled with coffee plantations, the next scaling rocky paths past snow-capped volcanoes. Like always, they would look for the right time to abandon their ride. They were able to dismount out of the truck and ended up by a group of small farms…

As they continued to make their way north, small farming villages dotted their path; workers would sometimes toss them vegetables or corn. Juanito would cautiously grab the corn or vegetables and share a bit with Ungér. He always kept an eye out though, as Ungér made him aware that carnitas was one of the favorite foods in Mexico. But fate shined on them, and they were allowed to find their way.

They also came across a few huge automobile factories built by those from the north. Factories that displaced many local farmers with the promise of prosperity… but alas, there was none… that prosperity seemed to make its way north also… leaving the workers with very little; forcing them on the same journey north as Juanito and his friends were on now.

After days, if not weeks, the three journey mates finally ended up in the *Chihuahua Desert* south of Texas and hopefully a bit closer to the not so mythical River of Nueces.

The Mexican sun beat down as Juanito, Ungér, and Zephyr entered the rugged terrain.

As early evening came, they were barely moving. Their journey through this country had gone reasonably well, except for a non-stop drought that left them dehydrated and exhausted.

"I spy with my little eye," Juanito began as his voice cracked from thirst, "something... brown."

Ungér rolled her eyes. "Let me guess. A rock? A dead bush? An endless stretch of dusty road?"

"You're no fun," Juanito pouted. "It was that brown patch of dirt over there. So different from all the other brown patches of dirt."

Zephyr, circling above, called down, "Less chatter, more movement; we need to find water soon. It is getting too dark."

Her warning was cut short by a whistling sound.

WHOOSH!!!! A tranquilizer dart shot past Ungér and stuck into the side of Juanito.

"Juanito!" Ungér exclaimed.

PING! A second dart hit Ungér but bounced off her heavy thick fleece. She glanced around but saw no one. Panic was in her eyes as Juanito began to wobble. The drug in the dart started to take effect and Juanito's eyes became heavy. He smiled at Ungér.

"Over there," Juanito slurred…

THUMP! Juanito's massive body tumbled to the ground, unconscious.

"Over where?" Ungér panicked. Before she could see what Juanito meant, she heard a man's voice in the dark.

"Stand back, Sarah," he ordered.

WOOOSH!

Zephyr swooped down to try and protect Ungér, and the dart hit her; but did not stick… but injured her wing.

"That was an Andean Condor I hit… how in the world…?" the man's voice exclaimed.

Ungér could not make out where he was.

"I will use a new one for that, that sheep?" he uttered to a young girl by his side.

WHOOSH! Another dart hit Ungér. This time it buried deep within her fleece. She wobbled like Juanito had. She noticed Zephyr flying overhead, but then soon fell to the ground also. Groggy, she made out a figure approaching… a man by the name of Dr. Martinez dressed in a khaki researcher uniform with an iPad.

He seemed confused as he lowered the tranquilizer gun. Next to him stood a young girl.

"What are they, Papi?" asked his ten-year-old daughter Sarah, adjusting her thick-rimmed glasses as she peered at the animals. Her father kept scrolling through the iPad.

"Nothing native to this area that's for sure, *mija.*" Dr. Martinez bent over and inspected Juanito closer. *"Ay, mi niña,* I think they are nothing more than a pig and a lost sheep," he said with surprise.

"What about that huge bird? I've never seen anything like it!" Sarah exclaimed, her eyes wide with wonder.

Dr. Martinez kept scrolling through his iPad. He scratched his head. "That's an Andean Condor, sweetheart. That pig is... not a wild boar... it resembles..." his voice tapered off. He looked at a picture of an Iberian pig on his iPad... "No way... out here in the Mexican desert?" he uttered. He just closed his iPad and focused on Ungér.

Ungér was fading fast. She could barely hear what they were saying... She eyed Zephyr who dived closer to them but swooped away as Dr. Martinez stepped protectively in front of Sarah. The last thing Ungér remembered was Dr. Martinez's voice.

“Too late to go back to the sanctuary tonight. Let's make camp and go first thing in the morning.” And with that Ungér fell completely asleep.

A frustrated Zephyr flew overhead in circles as Juanito and Ungér laid out on the desert floor next to a large cactus. Zephyr made sure she found a safe spot on top of a saguaro cactus and listened to every word the humans said.

“Poor creatures. They've clearly wandered far from where they belong. We need to get them to the sanctuary before they suffer any more in this harsh environment,” Dr. Martinez uttered.

“But Papi, how did they get all the way out here? There aren't any farms nearby,” Sarah wondered.

“That's exactly why we need to help them,” Dr. Martinez replied. “They clearly need our protection.”

The painted desert was completely dark. Ungér and Juanito lay sleeping on the colorful sand. Their peaceful sleep, such a contrast to all the turmoil on the trip to get to

this point. Dr. Martinez and Sarah made camp next to Juanito and Ungér.

Zephyr kept an eye on Juanito and Ungér as she continued to listen to the humans.

Dr. Martinez built a small fire, and Sarah helped arrange their camping supplies near their utility truck. On the side of the truck in big letters: '*Caridad* Animal Sanctuary.' Two large animal cages were on the back of the truck.

Dr. Martinez brought out a small guitar and started strumming it as he sat down next to the campfire. Sarah stirred a pot of her father's famous vegetable soup hanging over the fire.

"I am so tired, Papi. I can barely keep my eyes open," Sarah yawned.

"Me too, mija." Dr. Martinez returned the yawn. It has been a very long day. "Thanks for coming with me. I know how much you like animals," he smiled.

They did not notice that Juanito began to stir.

The serene scene, with stars staring down, twinkling in anticipation of a song, is what Juanito saw as he slowly opened his eyes... Ungér quickly followed. Juanito whispered to her.

"Don't move, Ungér... let me think."

Juanito scoured the horizon and finally spied Zephyr sitting on top of the large saguaro cactus. The full moon behind her and the brilliant starlit sky any other time would have been something Juanito would have enjoyed... but not tonight. He had no idea what was going on. He nodded to Zephyr, who nodded back. Juanito's glance encouraged her to wait.

Ungér and Juanito just kept their eye on the father and daughter...

Dr. Martinez started to sing songs about animals... "/...and maybe there will come a time... /... a time when we can frolic and play together.../"

"I love that song, Papi. Do you think animals and humans will ever really be friends?" Sarah asked, her eyes bright with hope.

Dr. Martinez eyed Juanito and Ungér, who pretended they were still asleep.

“I don't know, mija. But I think the most important thing is that we try. Try and make things right,” Dr. Martinez sighed.

Sarah ladled out two bowls of soup and couldn't take her eyes off Juanito and Ungér as she handed one to her father.

“That pig is so dark and huge. I've never seen anything like it,” she said with wonder.

“Animals are being displaced all over the world. Who knows what misfortune brought him here,” Dr. Martinez replied thoughtfully as he sipped his soup.

Ungér was becoming restless, Juanito whispered to her.

“They will be going to sleep soon, be patient,” he encouraged her.

Sarah eyed them both. They noticed and pretended to sleep again. Sarah thought she saw them move. “Papi, are they waking up?” Sarah wondered. Dr. Martinez eyed them.

“No, sweetheart. That was a pretty strong medicine I had to give them to keep them calm.”

He got up and went over and put a lasso-like rope over their necks. Juanito and Ungér did not move. Dr. Martinez secured them to a large cactus.

"It will be quite difficult to get that large pig in the truck; but we will worry about that tomorrow," he smiled. He went back over and sat by the fire. He strummed the guitar again... Sarah gazed up at the stars, then back at the animals, clutching a stuffed animal.

"Papi..." Sarah said softly, watching the animals with concern. "Why does it have to be this way?" she wondered aloud.

"What way?" he answered.

"It seems like more animals wander, lost, as farmers and others head north."

Dr. Martinez put down the guitar. "The farmers go north so they can make money, feed their famili—"

Sarah cut him off.

"But why can't they stay here in Mexico, or Honduras, Guatemala, or other places? There is such rich soil here," she stated.

"Years of economic chaos caused by the north and their associates," Dr. Martinez paused, not finishing his thought.

"What do you mean, ec-o-nomic chaos?" Sarah asked, confused by the phrase.

Dr. Martinez stared out at the starlit sky and then at the northern horizon... He then eyed his daughter. He rubbed his chin and scratched his hair. He wanted to describe the displacement in a way that would make sense to her…

… He leaned forward…

"It is like, they took a baseball bat to a beehive, stole all the honey, then wonder why the bees swarmed north?" Dr. Martinez let the visual metaphor sink into his daughter.

Dr. Martinez sighed and sang another song. Ungér and Juanito kept a watchful eye on both the doctor and Sarah as he sang. Dr. Martinez stopped playing and eyed the moonlit horizon in all directions.

"And some from here are not without blame either; they take advantage of uh, their plight… fuel their desperation," he paused, reflective. Then went on…

Sarah just nodded her head, listening trying to make sense of it all.

"Others turn to the cartels." Dr. Martinez lamented. "Yes, many feed from the shattered beehive," Dr. Martinez explained.

"I am sorry, mija," he sighed. "I talk of things you don't understand."

"I think there is much I need to learn," Sarah surmised.

"The important thing is you are curious," Dr. Martinez smiled. He kissed his daughter on her forehead. "And it's important that you do what you think is right; pursue <u>your</u> curiosity… not mine…"

Dr. Martinez gathered more pieces of mesquite firewood. He tossed some into the fire and the flames rose high into the air…

"There are not many predators that we need to worry about out here… but this will keep any critters away," he assured Sarah.

Juanito and Ungér bided their time as Dr. Martinez and Sarah talked around the campfire barely able to keep their eyes open. She eyed Juanito and Ungér.

"They seem so… natural in the wild. Do you think the sanctuary is really best for them?" Dr. Martinez smiled at his caring daughter.

"Unfortunately, there is no other place for them to go," Dr. Martinez sadly stated.

Juanito stared at Ungér and shook his head in disagreement. There was somewhere else they could go… that is if The River of Nueces did exist…

Finally… Dr. Martinez and Sarah pulled out separate sleeping bags and went to sleep on opposite sides of the flickering campfire.

As the doctor and Sarah fell into a deep sleep from their weariness, Juanito and Ungér quietly tried to free themselves with no success. Zephyr flew over and tried to peck at the rope.

"It's too thick. Maybe try to slip it over your heads," Zephyr whispered.

No such luck. They could not get free. Juanito was so frustrated. He pulled with all his weight but could not break free as he oinked.

"Careful, you will wake them." Zephyr whispered in Juanito's ear.

A rustle in the bushes made Juanito and Ungér tense.

"What is it Juanito?" Ungér asked.

"I don't know. Maybe it is that swarm of bees they were talking about," Juanito answered.

Though she was nervous, Ungér chuckled. "That was an example Juanito, that's all."

Juanito stayed focused on the bushes…

"They were talking about why everyone is headed north. Why everyone is leaving," Ungér explained.

"A beehive fell once in the Dehesa and bees were everywhere. I got stung on my butt-, uh, I mean uh, rear end…" Juanito lamented.

"You are missing the point, Juanito," Zephyr chimed in.

"Quiet! Both of you, you will wake them up!" Ungér whispered.

Something bolted out of the bushes!

But instead of another threat, they saw a scruffy, intelligent-looking coyote emerge.

Juanito sniffed the air, and the scent made him stare straight at the coyote.

"Who are you?" Ungér whispered, being careful not to wake the humans. But with hope in her voice.

"You speak my dialect? Good, so aren't you two in a pickle," the coyote said, his voice a husky whisper.

"Name's Coyotl," the coyote replied, working on the ropes with his teeth. "And I'm guessing you'd rather not be poked and probed by these science geeks."

"I'm Juanito and she's Ungér," Juanito kept his voice down. "I had enough poking by electric cattle prods in my short life already. So, no more poking for me, thank you, Coyotl," Juanito uttered.

"Let's get out of here before these wannabe do-gooders wake up." Coyotl pleaded.

Coyotl smiled and gestured for Juanito to follow him.

“I really don’t think they will hurt us. I think in their minds they think they are helping us. They seem like nice humans,” Juanito whispered.

“Nice, sure… with their sanctuaries and their good intentions,” Coyotl sarcastically disagreed. Coyotl began to pace. Living in the wild close to humans made Coyotl cautious.

This changing desert life kept him on edge. As they made their way away from the humans, Coyotl peeked back at the sleeping pair… deep in their dreamland.

“But they don't see the irony. They'll 'rescue' us from the very places we called home long before they built their cities here. Then they get angry when we try to survive in the concrete jungle they created,” Coyotl explained.

Coyotl hurried up to the top of a nearby small hill. He looked out at some far away city lights in the distance… “Funny how they call us invasive when we were here first.” Coyotl joked.

Zephyr swooped down with her not so injured wing. “Thank the winds for this *lobo chico*. Not only is he helpful, but he is quite insightful too,” she exclaimed.

“Your wing, Zephyr?” Juanito asked.

“Just a scratch,” Zephyr smirked.

Once they were far away from the camp, the group turned to Coyotl.

“We can't thank you enough,” Juanito said. “Why did you help us?”

Coyotl shrugged with a hint of sadness in his eyes. “Let's just say I know what it's like to be hunted. To be seen as nothing more than a nuisance or a meal or be studied like a science project.”

“You could come with us,” Ungér offered. “We're headed to a place called The River of Nueces. It's supposed to be a paradise.”

Coyotl's ears perked up but then drooped. “Ah, I've heard tales of the north. But every time I've tried to go that way; I'm met with nothin' but resistance and hate. Humans up there, they don't take too kindly to coyotes.”

“But it would be better than here,” Juanito pressed. “Where you have to sneak in the shadows.”

Coyotl shook his head and cast a wry smile. “You'd think so, wouldn't you? But here, at least, I know the score. I have got my wits, my freedom, and the occasional chance to help some interesting folks like yourselves. It ain't much, but it's home.”

Zephyr, who had been quiet for a while, said, “I understand, Coyotl. Sometimes, where we feel we belong isn't always where others think we should be.”

Coyotl nodded appreciatively. “Exactly, winged sister. You get it.”

As the first light of dawn began to color the sky, they knew it was time to part ways.

“You sure we can't convince you?” Juanito asked one last time.

Coyotl chuckled. “Nah, but I appreciate the offer. You all take care of each other, you hear? The world needs more friendships like yours.”

Ungér nuzzled Coyotl. “Thank you, Coyotl. We won't forget you.”

Juanito studied Coyotl. He could not help but think about Paulo and how they left because they knew where they must go... where they must be. He thought the same about Coyotl. He declined to join them on their journey to The River of Nueces, because he thought he was exactly where he should be. He could help others better by staying in the desert to help those in distress. But Juanito knew his destiny was still in front of him.

As Coyotl turned to leave, he called over his shoulder, "Oh, and if you see any road runners up north, tell them Coyotl says hello. They'll know what it means."

Coyotl hurried away back towards the campsite to make sure Dr. Martinez and Sarah were still asleep. But he froze as Sarah stirred and looked in his direction. She noticed the three journey mates were gone also. She reached toward her father but couldn't keep her eyes off of Coyotl. He seemed to smile at her and put his paw to his mouth as if to say: Shhhh! Sarah smiled back and held her stuffed animal tight. She put her finger to her mouth as if to return the 'Shhhh…' Coyotl nodded to her again and started to move away… He stopped and noticed that Sarah put her head back down on the sleeping bag and went back to sleep… With that, he smiled again and disappeared into the desert brush as the trio were barely visible in the distance and continued on their journey north.

A sea of sand and rock in the painted desert stretched out before them. Juanito, Ungér, and Zephyr trudged along. As they crested a small hill, a forest of towering saguaro cacti came into view, their silhouettes stark against the mid-morning sun.

With a smile tugging at his lips, Juanito glanced at Ungér. “You know, your wool's almost all grown back. It's nice to see you looking like yourself again.”

Ungér chuckled as she shook her coat. A small cloud of dust rose around her. “Well, I am not sure I have ever been this dirty. But yes, it is good to have my fleece back.”

She eyed Juanito's sweater, now tattered and stained from their long journey. “Don't you think it's time to take that off? It must be sweltering in this heat.”

“No, I... I would rather keep it on,” Juanito said. His eyes met Ungér's, conveying more than his words. “It means too much to me.”

Ungér's expression softened, understanding the unspoken sentiment.

The day lingered on, and they made substantial progress. No sign of predators or of Dr. Martinez pursuing them.

Late in the day Zephyr descended and landed beside Juanito and Ungér.

“Well, my friends,” the condor said, stretching her wings, “I think it's time we call it a day. These old wings need a rest, and this looks like a good spot to spend the night.”

They settled in the shadow of another giant saguaro cactus. The sky above them slowly turned into a glittering canvas of stars, more numerous and brilliant than they had ever seen.

“It's beautiful,” Ungér breathed, her eyes wide with wonder. “Like something out of a dream,” she exhaled.

Juanito nodded, awestruck. “I never knew the sky could hold so many stars.”

Zephyr chuckled. “Oh, you should see it from up there. It's like swimming in a sea of diamonds.” With that, Zephyr took flight to circle in the moonlit, star-studded sky, leaving Juanito and Ungér to talk.

"Oh, and speaking of dreams," Juanito said softly, "you never told me why you came back that day, Ungér."

"What do dreams have to do with any of that?" Ungér initially pondered.

She then noticed that Juanito smiled at her and became serious.

… He sighed and thought back to when Ungér left…

"I felt so strange that day. When I saw the two rams butting heads, I wanted to confront them. Use my hindquarters to knock both away. Show them that I was… just as worthy of your affection," Juanito stammered.

"Oh, Juanito… we are from two different worlds… you know we could never—"

"Oh, I know, I know… it's just… this friendship thing is so hard sometimes," Juanito exhaled.

Ungér was quiet for a moment, watching the stars wheel overhead. She had avoided talking to Juanito about that day, but she knew she must.

“The flock was everything I thought I wanted. A family, little lambs of my own someday.” She turned to look at him. “But standing there, watching you leave, it felt wrong.”

“Wrong how?” Juanito asked.

“Sometimes what we think we want isn't what truly makes us happy,” Ungér explained. “I realized that true happiness comes from being with those who care about us, not just having what we think we need.”

Ungér moved closer to Juanito…

“Maybe, if we make it to The River of Nueces, I can find a flock and we can still stay friends? I knew I couldn’t have that if I stayed with that other flock,” Ungér sighed.

“You always being my friend, would be the best!” exclaimed Juanito.

“I really owe you Ungér. You stayed by my side from the beginning… and you came back after you had everything you wanted…” Juanito explained.

Ungér’s moist eyes slowly rose up to Juanito.

“Not everything, Juanito,” she paused… She moved a bit closer to Juanito.

"… I no longer had your friendship…" she confessed.

Juanito was deeply moved by the words. He didn't know where to look, but then finally stared into her eyes.

"You will always be my friend, Ungér, no matter what," Juanito assured her.

Ungér affectionately nudged Juanito's tattered sweater. "Besides, who else would appreciate your terrible jokes?"

Juanito chuckled. "I am quite funny, aren't I?"

"I wouldn't go that far," her voice grew lighter.

They lay in silence, the desert wind whispering around them.

"Well," Juanito finally said, "I'm glad… glad you came back."

"So am I," Ungér whispered. After a pause, she added, "And who knows? Maybe there will be a flock waiting at The River of Nueces. If it's meant to be."

Juanito smiled. "The best journeys have unexpected destinations and outcomes."

The thought lingered in the air as the two of them just stared up at the moonlit sky. They were so different, yet so similar. Their dreams connected them. But more importantly their friendship bonded them together; they both realized how precious and unique it really was.

Juanito reflected on how he had become such close friends with Zephyr and Ungér. How they had become so important to him, just as Conejo used to be. He was not sure why, but at that moment he thought about how Conejo had once told him: 'True friends try to help each other out.' The words Conejo said so long ago to Juanito, now rang so true to him. Friendship was about being there for someone. Juanito was so glad his friend Zephyr and Ungér were there for him. He could not take his eyes off of… Ungér…

Zephyr returned from her short flight.

As they all gazed at the celestial display, Juanito's stomach growled. He looked at his companions before turning his attention to the cactus. With careful precision, he began to bite off chunks.

"Here," he said, offering the juicy pulp to Zephyr. "You should eat first. You've been flying all day."

Zephyr blinked in surprise but accepted the morsels. Juanito turned to Ungér, presenting her with another piece. "You too, Ungér. You need to keep up your strength."

Juanito only took a piece after his friends had eaten and drank their fill of cactus juice. As he chewed, he noticed Zephyr and Ungér exchanged glances and smiles.

"What?" he asked, confused. "Do I have cactus stuck in my teeth or something?"

Ungér shook her head, and her eyes twinkled. "No, Juanito. I'm just... Well, I am proud of you."

"Proud of me? For what?"

"When I first met you, well, let's say you thought of yourself first. And now look at you," Ungér continued. "Making sure we eat before you do, always checking if we're okay. You've become quite the selfless pig."

Juanito felt a warmth that had nothing to do with the desert heat. "I... I had not thought about it. I want to take care of you both. You're my family now."

Juanito nosed the ground with his snout, then stared out at the horizon. “I have learned so much since I left the Dehesa,” Juanito sighed.

Ungér turned her head, curious but supportive.

“Conejo tried to show me how my selfishness was so harmful to others. How I took advantage of others less fortunate by hording all the acorns. Now, it all makes so much sense. I have seen how the same type of behavior by others has hurt so many on this journey of ours,” Juanito lamented.

An uncomfortable silence fell over the group, broken by the whisper of the wind through the cacti. Juanito shifted, and Ungér changed the subject.

“You know, Juanito,” she said, “you've lost quite a bit of weight on this journey.”

Relieved, Juanito looked down at himself. “I have, haven't I? You could say I'm bringing home the leaner bacon now.”

Juanito primped a bit, to show off his new physique, then grinned, “My belly doesn't jiggle like jelly anymore, does it?”

Ungér just shook her head at him and chuckled…

As the night grew later their conversation shifted from memories of their journey to hopes for the future. Zephyr straightened her wings as her keen eyes scanned the horizon.

“You know,” she said, her voice filled with excitement, “I think we must be close to The River of Nueces now. Because of the wind, it's different here.”

Juanito perked up. “Different, how?”

Zephyr spread her wings, feeling the air currents. “It's warmer. Softer, somehow. I've never been this far north in all my years of flying. But I have heard tales of this wind. They call it the breath of the north.”

Ungér's eyes shone with hope. “Do you think we're almost there?”

Zephyr nodded. “I do. First thing in the morning, I will fly ahead and scout. If I'm right, we could reach The River of Nueces by nightfall tomorrow.”

Juanito was reflective. After all they'd been through, their destination seemed to be within reach. “I can't wait to see it,” he said, his voice hushed with anticipation. “I wonder if it will be like I imagine. A place where we can all find what we want; find ourselves. Do you think it'll be everything we've dreamed of?”

Ungér leaned against him. “I don't know, Juanito. I think my dreams have changed.”

“What do you mean, changed?” Juanito asked.

“Well, now that we shared this journey together, my dreams include your dreams, and Zephyr’s dream too. I just want it to be a place where we can all find happiness together,” Ungér stated.

Zephyr nodded in agreement. As they settled in for the night, the stars twinkled above like silent guardians; Juanito felt a deep sense of peace.

No matter the challenges…

… He knew he could face anything with Ungér and Zephyr by his side…

Chapter 9:
The Final Push

Acorn of wisdom:

Texas has more species of oak trees than any place in North America.

As sleep claimed them, their dreams were filled with visions of flowing waters, abundant food, and the freedom they'd fought so hard to find.

The first rays of dawn touched the desert sky when Zephyr moved as her keen eyes blinked open. She nudged Juanito and Ungér awake.

"Come on, sleepyheads," she whispered, her voice tinged with excitement and a hint of pain. "We need to start moving."

Juanito yawned. “How's your wing, Zephyr? Think you can fly today?”

Zephyr stretched her wings. “I can manage short bursts, but I won't be able to scout ahead as I'd hoped. Still, The River of Nueces must be close. I can feel it in my feathers.”

They set off, hope driving their weary bodies forward. Minutes seemed like hours, and the hours seemed like days. The desert seemed more unforgiving than ever, the sun beating down on their backs. Juanito's tongue felt like sandpaper in his mouth, and Ungér's wool was matted with sweat and dust.

“Water,” Ungér bleated, her eyes squinted against the glare. “I'd give anything for just a drop of water.”

Ungér remembered the herbs the older woman in the Andes, Chaska, stuffed in her remaining wool. She shook, and the small pouch with the moist herbs fell to the ground. Ungér chewed on the pouch strings and herbs scattered onto the desert floor. They were so wet they formed mini puddles of water.

Zephyr swooped down and partook. Ungér and Juanito smiled at each other and licked up the tiny puddles one after the next until they could drink no more.

Juanito nodded to Zephyr who was back in the sky above them and then to Ungér.

Juanito looked back in the direction of where the Andes rested so far away and acknowledged the older woman who had helped them.

"Thank you, Chaska…" is all he said as they hurried on their way.

Hours passed, with each step more difficult than the last. Just as they were about to give up hope, Zephyr cried from above.

"There! There it is!"

Juanito and Ungér looked up. Shimmering in the distance like a mirage, a line of green cut through the barren landscape next to a crystal blue river.

So, after months of the most grueling and difficult journey, Juanito and his loyal comrades finally reached their long-sought destination.

“The River of Nueces,” Juanito breathed as his heart pounded. “It does exist!”

As they drew closer, they made out lush vegetation, towering nut trees, and even a few cattle grazing. Rabbits darted between bushes, reminding Juanito of his old friend. It truly was magical, mystical not in a fantasy way, but in a tangible way.

Each color seemed more vibrant; each chirp of the birds seemed angelic. Rows and rows of colorful corn, watermelons, squash, tomatoes went on and on.

The inviting green meadow was covered with acorns and pecans as far as the eye could see… and a babbling gentle river with serene blue ponds covered with ducks and geese… Juanito closed his eyes and shook his head to make sure he wasn’t dreaming.

…. He wasn’t…

Juanito thought of the long journey and reality that laid in front of him. He thought of Lorenzo and how his pursuit fueled the urgency to get where he was. He felt sad for Lorenzo. He remembered the conversation with Santiago and how there was so much sadness in Lorenzo’s early life. He thought maybe that is what made Lorenzo so blind to the pain of those around him… maybe Lorenzo would have been different if his mother had not died… Juanito sighed and then thought of Conejo and shed a tear.

"Conejo would have loved this," he whispered, a bittersweet smile on his face. Ungér noticed how happy Juanito was as he reminisced about his old friend…

"True friendship never dies. It lives on in our hearts and actions," Ungér nodded.

Ungér nuzzled him. "I never knew your friend, but I know he'd be proud of you, Juanito." Their joy was clear as they reached the water's edge. But before they could take a drink…

… Suddenly… like an ominous dark cloud…

Three powerful figures appeared from the undergrowth, their stance hostile and unwelcoming. A massive buffalo named Bubba stepped forward, his bulk casting a long shadow in the morning light. Next to him were Cletus, a Texas Longhorn steer with impressive horns that gleamed, and Skeeter, a stern-looking Bald Eagle who perched on a nearby branch with wings partially spread in an intimidating display.

“Hold it right there,” Bubba drawled, his deep voice carrying an edge of threat. “We're protectors of the Southern Soil.”

Cletus stomped at the ground, angry. “Yeah, we don't need your kind here anymore.” Behind him, in the fields were former farmers and workers from the countries Juanito and his friends passed through to get to The River of Nueces. The workers stacked bales of alfalfa hay; the same alfalfa that Cletus chewed on, the irony lost on him.

The three border bullies formed a wall between the travelers and the water. Bubba's massive form blocked most of the path, while Cletus waved his enormous horns back and forth. Skeeter's sharp eyes missed nothing from his perch.

Juanito whispered to Ungér, “What an unfriendly welcome. Nothing says 'paradise' quite like a grumpy, babbling buffalo.”

But beneath his attempt at humor, Juanito felt his temper rise. All they had endured; Lorenzo's pursuit, the freezing mountains, the scorching deserts… only to face this? He stepped forward, his voice carrying the weight of their journey.

"We have traveled thousands of kilometers and faced countless dangers, all for the dream of a better life. And this is how you greet us?"

Cletus snorted loudly. "We don't take in outsiders around these parts."

Juanito tilted his head thoughtfully. In Cletus's features, he recognized the same characteristics as the bulls he had known on the Dehesa. His voice softened with understanding.

"Outsiders? That is curious, my Longhorn friend. Your ancestors and mine shared the same Spanish meadows once. The same warm sun, the same sweet grass."

The observation seemed to unsettle Cletus. His tail swished nervously. "Things are different now."

"Different?" Juanito's voice carried a new edge. He moved closer to Cletus, his gaze sweeping over the paradise they had sought for so long. He thought of all they had seen. Of the large commercial farms replacing smaller ones, the logging, the deforestation. He couldn't take his eyes off the path they had traveled from the south.

… His voice grew stronger with conviction.

“So, what is different is outsiders from here took everything they wanted from down there.” Juanito nodded toward the migrant workers. “You’ve taken everything from them… their land, their crops and their resources, even their labor… and *now* you close the door?”

The words struck home. Cletus's eyes flashed not just with anger, but with the fury of one whose certainties had been shaken. The tension in the air became electric.

Bubba stepped forward in support of Cletus. “You best watch your tone, porky.” Bubba eyed Skeeter and Cletus. “We just trying to protect our families; protect what is rightfully ours.” The three border bullies nodded in agreement.

But Juanito stood his ground. “Rightfully yours? How do you figure?” Juanito waddled back and forth and mocked them. “Why, because you are the biggest and strongest? It’s the natural order-” Juanito cut himself off. He stared out at one of the rabbits remembering he had said the same thing to Conejo so long ago to justifying hoarding all the acorns from the helpless piglets.

Zephyr landed beside Juanito; wings spread protectively. "We mean no harm. We only seek shelter; for much of mine in the Andes has been destroyed by many from here."

Juanito moved in front of each of the Southern Soil guards. He took in the migrant workers in the distance, glanced at Zephyr alongside him, and finally eyed Ungér before locking eyes with Cletus… there was a resolve in Juanito's eyes that Ungér had never seen before. Ungér moved between Cletus and Juanito, her wool bristled with worry.

"Juanito, don't—"

She tried to push Juanito back, but Juanito offered up one more verbal wisdom for Cletus and the others to chew on….

"Why must hate build walls when friendship can build bridges?" Juanito challenged the border trio. "We're full up," Skeeter shrugged.

"But how do we get by, when you've already taken everything we need back home?" Zephyr asked. Cletus's breathing became heavy, his nostrils flared. The truth in the three journey mates' words seemed to enrage him further.

Ungér pushed Juanito aside and got eye to eye with Cletus.

“Same old story. Take what you want, then slam the door shut and call it yours,” Ungér exclaimed.

Cletus backed up and scraped the ground with his hoof. He lowered his horns and tossed them side to side. He glared at Ungér with his nostrils flaring.

“That's it, Fleece Face! You and your flea-bitten friends go back to where you came from!” He charged…

“Cletus, stop!” Skeeter's voice rang out in protest. But Cletus was already in motion… Time seemed to slow…

Juanito saw Cletus’s horns aimed straight at Ungér. Without hesitation, Juanito threw himself in front of Ungér.

The impact was devastating. Cletus's horn caught Juanito in his side, piercing through his cherished sweater. For just a moment, Juanito's eyes met Ungér's, and in that gaze was everything he had never said to her. Then Cletus's fury sent Juanito flying into the trunk of an oak tree with a sickening CRACK!

“Juanito!” Ungér's scream echoed across the water.

Skeeter eyed Cletus with disdain. He stared at Juanito and then over The River of Nueces at the migrant workers in the nearby alfalfa field.

"We are... better than this," Skeeter sadly stated.

The words hung in the air; their power changed the demeanor of a now regretful Cletus.

... All eyes turned to Ungér who kneeled on her two-front legs over Juanito.

"Why, Juanito?" she sobbed. "Why did you do that?"

Juanito smiled, and teary-eyed, said more than any words could. He seemed to understand his fate. A certain peace came over him. He could only think of Ungér. The selfish Juanito left a long time ago... he just kept staring at Ungér...

"Ungér," Juanito whispered, his voice growing fainter. "You never told me... your real name." Through her tears, Ungér pressed close to him. "Oh, Juanito... to you, I'll always be Ungér, your friend."

... Juanito was beginning to slip away... his eyes heavy… but not his smile.

"Friend… yes, I like that. I will remember you as 'Ungér' my 'friend' if you will," Juanito labored.

Ungér sighed and nudged closer to Juanito. "Juanito you will always be my friend, my very best friend… always."

Juanito was fading fast... so fast that Ungér could not get her head around it all…

… But Juanito could…

A ripple of sunlight crossed Juanito's face. "Friend..." he breathed. He said it like he was taking in each letter as he spoke to his dear Ungér. "You truly have been my best friend."

Ungér pressed close, tears streamed down her face. "Please don't leave, Juanito."

Gasping for his last breath, Juanito's smile would not fade. "It was all worth it, my friend," he whispered. Then with moist eyes he implored Ungér…

"Show them, Ungér... show them... love... conquers... fear."

The powerful words hung in the air. It was as if everyone on both sides were taking them in. Zephyr landed beside them; her eyes filled with sorrow. And in a show of support for Ungér, unfurled her wings.

Ungér's sorrow transformed into a burning determination as she eyed Juanito. She then turned to face Bubba, Cletus, and Skeeter with a new sense of fury.

“Do you see what you've done?” her voice cracked with emotion.

Tears streamed down her face as she continued, her words directed at Cletus. “He threw himself in front of your horns to protect me. That's the kind of friend Juanito was… I mean is,” Ungér's voice trailed off as Juanito’s eyes closed.

Ungér's gaze swept over all three of the border bullies. “We're not so different, you know. We all want safety, friendship; a place to belong. Is that too much to ask?”

She looked down at Juanito's still form but her tears could not wash away the truth...

... Juanito was gone...

“Juanito’s last wish was for this place to be where we could all coexist.” Ungér tearfully uttered. Ungér looked up from Juanito and focused on the three powerful figures that blocked their way.

Bubba seemed the most uncomfortable. He roared loud grunts and bellowed deep gut-wrenching snorts over and over.

“If you'd have stayed where you came from, none of this would have happened,” Bubba whined.

Ungér's fierce glare received a supportive glance from Cletus and Skeeter. They were changing, even if Bubba wasn't.

“Believe me, you don't want a piece of me, missy,” Bubba snorted.

Ungér was unfazed by the mammoth Bubba, who snorted even louder and scraped the ground with his hoof as if he were going to charge. He even tried to raise up on two legs, but of course, he couldn’t.

Ungér stood her ground in front of him. “I'm not afraid of you... you... blundering beast! You are nothing more than a scared bully.”

Ungér backed up and ran at full speed ahead toward Bubba and, to everyone's surprise, the much smaller sheep head-butted the mammoth buffalo.

Like most bullies, Bubba was not as tough as he acted.

Frightened and embarrassed, Bubba eyed a regretful Cletus and Skeeter and just ran off.

… Bubba was never to be seen again…

The remorseful Cletus and Skeeter took a step back as shame and sorrow etched on their faces. Ungér proceeded to verbally throttle Cletus.

"Again, I ask; do you havc any idca what you've done?" she cried, tears streaming down her face. "Juanito was my best friend. He was kind and selfless. He dreamed of a better world where we could all peacefully live together. And now he's gone... because of ignorance and fear."

Ungér's voice carried across the water and echoed off the distant hills. The silence between them all spoke more than any words could.

Cletus was stunned, unable to shake the guilt for what he had done.

They all stood beside the great oak where Juanito had fallen; their heads lowered out of respect. Ungér sobbed over her friend. The best friend she ever had... her Juanito... who always encouraged her and supported her...

… and yes… now he was gone...

Chapter 10:

Epilogue -The Legacy of Juanito...

Acorn of wisdom:

The mightiest oak tree grows not from the largest acorn, but from the one planted with the greatest love.

As the weeks passed, months turned into a year and then two... and The River of Nueces became the animal sanctuary that Juanito had dreamed of…

... Ungér made sure of that...

… The once sentimental wanderer, was now the *matriarch* of The River of Nueces…

This typical morning would have made Juanito smile. The sun rose over The River of Nueces in shades of pink, gold, and lavender. The once-barren landscape around the oasis of The River of Nueces, transformed into a lush paradise filled with life and harmony. The air filled with the sweet scent of wildflowers and the gentle music of rustling leaves and flowing water.

Zephyr perched atop an ancient oak tree, her feathers gleaming in the morning light. She was surrounded by a mini flock of condors who migrated to the sanctuary. Below them in the lush meadows were familiar faces… descendants of the animals who once stood against newcomers, now were part of this diverse community.

Nestled in the branches around Zephyr, hatched condor chicks chirped, with their mothers nearby, their downy feathers ruffling in the gentle breeze. A large male condor eyed the beauty of the bountiful fields of fruits and vegetables below. The condor bowed his head to Zephyr in a gesture of respect. He then eyed the young condor chicks.

"Little ones, listen to your, uh, Auntie Zephyr," he exclaimed. Zephyr nodded respectfully back to the condor and his mate, the mother of the chicks.

Zephyr stepped onto a branch, surveying the vast oasis of the River of Nueces. She took a deep breath… then, her voice soared on the wind.

"Look upon this land and know that it was born from a dream. A dream of belonging, of acceptance, a world where all creatures could live together peacefully."

The chicks quieted down, captivated by Zephyr's words. They eyed the meadow below and animals of all shapes as they roamed free. Rabbits hopped alongside deer, while buffalo grazed next to a family of *Javelina.* Near the riverbank, a pack of coyotes played with a pack of wolves, their long-forgotten past rivalries not even a memory.

... Pecan trees and oak trees spanned endlessly into the horizon...

"This paradise," Zephyr continued, "was made possible by the sacrifice of a remarkable friend: an Iberian pig named Juanito. He taught us that true strength lies not in our differences but in our ability to come together despite the differences."

All eyes turned toward some free-range cattle, horses, and other animals, who led a few humans that were all heading south, away from The River of Nueces. A young condor, confusion in their eyes, turned to Zephyr.

"Why are they leaving, Auntie Zephyr?" the young bird asked.

Zephyr smiled as she watched them go. "They are going south to try and help others restore some of the farms that were taken from them, so they don't have to travel north to have their own River of Nueces. Some will help our friend Paulo, help restore the rainforest too," Zephyr explained.

In a soft, grassy hollow near the base of an ancient oak tree, Ungér snuggled close to a robust and handsome ram named Arlo. Around them, three fluffy lambs frolicked in the morning dew. Ani, the smallest of the lambs, stopped, and her attention was drawn to something on the ground.

"Mama," Ani bleated and nudged a small, oval object with her nose. "What's this? It looks yummy, but I can't eat it."

Ungér's eyes softened as she studied the acorn. She nuzzled her confused lamb offspring. "That my dear, is an acorn. And while it may not be food for us, it holds an extraordinary meaning."

"Oh, does it remind you of your friend Juanito who is no longer with us?" Ani inquired. A moist-eyed Ungér took the acorn with her teeth and gently set it on top of a large rock in the middle of them all. She stared at the acorn, and she smiled.

"My child, Juanito, is still with us," Ungér said, her voice soft, but strong. "I feel him in every breeze that whispers through these trees. I see him in every act of kindness between old enemies turned friends. I hear his laughter in the rustle of leaves, his wisdom in the falling acorns."

The other lambs, Lilit and Aram, gathered around, their curiosity piqued by their mother's tone. Sensing the moment's importance, Arlo moved closer to his family. "Maybe it is time you told them the story of your great adventure."

Ungér nodded with a gentle smile on her face. "Yes, my darlings. It's time you heard the full tale." She took a deep breath, her voice taking on a very respectful tone. "Long ago, before you were born, I made an incredible journey with an extraordinary friend..."

As Ungér began her tale, a young Longhorn calf ambled over and was followed by his mother. The calf, named

Tanner, was the perfect likeness to his father, Cletus, but his eyes held none of the old suspicion – only curiosity and friendliness.

"Mind if we listen too, Ms. Ungér?" Tanner asked. "Before Pa died, he always talked about the brave pig who changed everything. He felt so bad for what happened."

Ungér smiled warmly. "Tanner, what we all do going forward is what's important." Tanner moseyed over next to Ani, nudged her, and smiled.

A young bald eagle named Whipper, indeed the offspring of Skeeter, landed next to Ungér. "I want to hear too, Ms. Ungér, please?"

Ungér stared at all the animals enjoying the blissful paradise... all of them sharing the beautiful tapestry of corn, grasslands, pecan trees and yes, the acorns from the mighty oaks.

Ungér focused on the acorn she put on top of the large rock… the morsel that meant so much to Juanito. "Sometimes the long way around… is the shortest way home," she whispered to herself.

… She was finally home… The home they all wanted, and she and Zephyr now enjoyed… without Juanito… Or maybe he was there… but just in a different way… She peeked over at the nearby oak tree…

There on its huge trunk hung Juanito's old wool sweater. While it was tattered and faded, Ungér looked at it a bit closer than usual…

Any signs of how Juanito had met his demise was gone… It just had the tapestry of stories intact just as before.

Ungér always thought it was strange how the tapestry had depicted their journey, even though Chaska, the older Peruvian woman knew very little of them. She eyed the sweater a bit closer and couldn't help notice so much more…

The sweater was filled with everyone they had met on the journey… and some Ungér did not recognize at first. In a distant Dehesa stood a smiling rabbit along with many of their siblings… As she looked closer, she smiled, surely that was the one Juanito called… Conejo.

As Ungér studied the sweater, it almost seemed to come alive…

Santiago was smiling in a field planting corn next to a large coffee plantation. Chaska was surrounded by culpeo foxes, vicuñas, and furry mountain rabbits. She was waving as if she stared straight at Ungér.

… And there was…

Paulo… back in the Amazon working alongside Mona, with her young offspring. The tapirs were there also, busy nudging rotting timber out of the way with their strong elephant style trunks… and there were a few humans… all working together to replant trees…

And behold, in the lower corner, there appeared the likeness of Lorenzo Valdez. Not cocky or flamboyant, but with a humble smile and a bowed head of respect.

… But what caught Ungér's eye the most, what made her tear up…

There on the sweater, as clear as day, was The River of Nueces… It looked exactly as it did now, with Ungér and Arlo and her three lamb children… Zephyr, who Chaska had never seen was displayed in the tree, just as she was now.

What made Ungér finally shed a large tear was… the image of Juanito there on the sweater… massive, dark, unmistakable. Smiling down on them.

Was Ungér just imagining all that? Was the image of Juanito really there? Was the full journey and all the others on display in the sweater?

… It didn't matter…

The journey was vivid in Ungér's mind. All the animals from The River of Nueces moved over towards Ungér… Ungér tearfully moved them closer…

… She took one more look at Juanito's sweater...

… "Gather 'round..." Ungér began...

… "There once was an Iberian pig named…"

… "Juanito..."

THE END

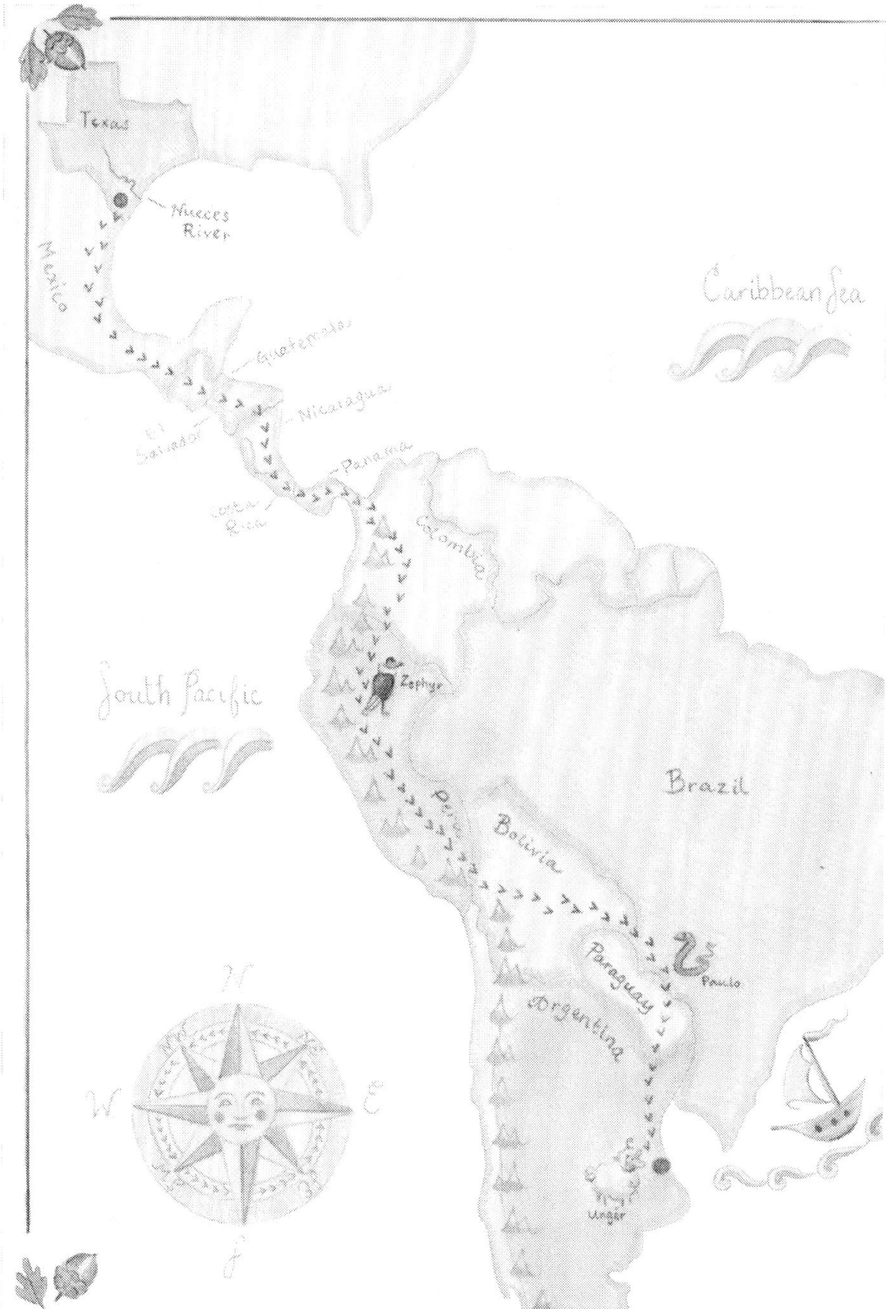
Texas
Nueces River
Mexico
Guatemala
Nicaragua
El Salvador
Panama
Costa Rica
Colombia
Caribbean Sea
Zephyr
South Pacific
Brazil
Peru
Bolivia
Paraguay
Paulo
Argentina
Ungar
N
W
E
S

Spain
Route from Spain to Argentina
Africa
South Atlantic

Alphabetical Glossary:

Acai berries (ah-sah-WE bare-ees) A purple rainforest fruit from South America.

Acorn (AY-korn) A nut or fruit of an oak tree used as food by many animals.

Agave (uh-GAH-vay) A desert plant used to make various products.

Alfalfa (al-FAL-fah) A plant grown as hay for feeding livestock.

Altiplano (al-tee-PLAH-no) A high plateau region in Bolivia and Peru.

Amazon (AM-uh-zon) The world's largest rainforest.

Andes (AN-deez) A massive mountain range along South America's western coast.

Arachis (uh-RAK-is) Wild peanut plant native to South America.

Argentina (ar-jen-TEE-na) Country in South America. Where Juanito meets Ungér.

Armenia (ar-MEEN-yah) A country in Asia, homeland of Ungér's ancestors.

Ayo (AH-you) Armenian word meaning “yes.”

Ayoreo (ay-oh-RAY-oh) Indigenous people of the Gran Chaco region.

Baaa (BAH) The sound a sheep makes.

Barbacoa (bar-bah-COH-ah) A traditional Mexican method of cooking meat.

Barev (bah-REV) **Im** (im) **Ungér** (OON-ker) Armenian way of saying: hello, my friend.

Blue-throated Macaw (BLOO-throh-ted muh-KAW) Blue and yellow Bolivian parrot.

Bolivia (boh-LIV-ee-ah) A South American country the friends pass through.

BoPaBra (BOP-eh-brah) Brazil-Paraguay-Bolivia border.

Brazil (bruh-ZIL): The largest country in South America.

Brazil nuts (bruh-ZIL nuts) Large seeds from South American rainforest trees.

Buenos Aires (BWEN-os AYE-res) The capital city of Argentina.

Caiman (KAY-min): A predatory reptile similar to an alligator.

Caña (KAH-nyah) A type of alcoholic beverage.

Capuchin (KAP-yoo-chin) A monkey species found in Central and South America.

Caridad (KARI'ðað) Spanish word meaning "charity."

Carneada (kar-nay-AH-dah) A traditional way of preparing meat in Latin America.

Carnitas (kar-NEE-tas) A Mexican dish made from pork.

Cartel (kahr-TEL) A group of organizations that control prices and limit competition.

Cassava (kə-SAH-və) A starchy root vegetable used as a food in tropical regions.

Ceiba (SAY-bah) A sacred tree species in Central America.

Central America (sen-trul uh-MAIR-i-ka) Region between North and South America.

Chaska (CHAS-ka) Quechua word meaning "star."

Che (cheh) Armenian word meaning "no."

Chechil (cheh-CHEEL) A type of Armenian string cheese.

Chihuahua Desert (chee-WAH-wah DEH-zert) A desert region in Mexico and the U.S.

Chorizo (chor-EE-zo) A type of spicy Spanish or Mexican sausage.

Choripan (chor-ee-PAN) A popular South American sandwich made with chorizo.

Chuño (CHOON-yo) Traditional Andean freeze-dried potatoes.

Churro (CHUR-oh) Fried dough pastry coated with sugar.

Cicadas (sih-KAY-duhs) Insects known for their buzzing sounds.

Coati (koh-AH-tee) – A raccoon-like mammal with a long snout and ringed tail

Coca (KOH-kah) A plant grown in South America.

Cochino (koh-CHEE-no) a pig, swine

Coco River (KOH-koh RIH-ver) forms the border between Honduras and Nicaragua.

Cocoa (KOH-koh) Seeds used to make chocolate.

Colombia (koh-LUM-bee-ah) A South American country known for diverse landscapes.

Compadres (kom-PAH-drays) Spanish word meaning "friends" or "companions."

Condor (KON-dor) A large bird of prey found in the Andes Mountains.

Conejo (koh-NAY-ho) Spanish word meaning "rabbit."

Conquistadors (kon-KEES-tuh-dorz) Spanish conquerors of the Americas.

Copán (koh-PAHN) Ancient Mayan ruins in Honduras.

Costa Rica (koh-stah REE-kah) Central American country known for beautiful beaches.

Coyotl (koy-OHT-ul) Nahuatl word for coyote.

Culinary (KUHL-uh-nair-ee) Relating to cooking or kitchen activities.

Culpeo (KOOL-pay-oh) An Andean fox species.

Cumbia (KOOM-bee-ah) A trendy style of Latin American music and dance.

Darién (dar-ee-EN) A dense jungle region in Panama.

Dehesa (day-HAY-sah) A special type of Spanish forest where animals roam freely.

Dios mío (dee-OS mee-OH) Spanish phrase meaning "my God."

Don (DOHN) A Spanish title of respect.

El Salvador (el sal-va-DOR) A country in Central America.

Epiphyte (EP-uh-fyte) A plant that grows on other plants without taking nutrients.

Gata (GAH-tah) A traditional Armenian sweet bread.

Gaucho (GOW-cho) Traditional Argentine cowboys.

Gran Chaco (gran CHA-ko) A large wilderness region in South America.

Guatemala (gwah-teh-MAH-lah) A Central American country.

Guatemalan Fir (gwah-teh-MAH-lan FUR) A species of pine tree native to Guatemala.

Hijo (EE-ho) Spanish word meaning "son" or "child."

Honduras (hon-DUR-as) A country in Central America.

Howler monkey (HOW-ler MON-ky) A large monkey known for its loud roar.

Iberian (eye-BEER-ee-an) Something from the Iberian Peninsula.

Jabiru stork (jab-uh-ROO) South American stork with black head and red neck pouch.

Jamón ibérico (ha-MON eye-BEAR-ee-co) A special type of cured ham from Spain.

Javelina (ha-veh-LEE-nah) A wild pig-like animal native to the Americas.

Kapok tree (KAY-pok tree) A large tropical tree found in the Amazon.

Llanos de Moxos (YANOS ðe ˈmoxos) A vast savanna in northern Bolivia.

Lobizón (low-bee-ZONE) A mythical werewolf-like creature from South America.

Lobo Chico (LOH-boh CHEE-koh) A Coyote-like animal.

Mahogany (mah-HOG-any) A valuable tropical hardwood tree.

Matriarch (MAY-tree-ahrk) A female leader of a family or group.

Mexico (MEH-hee-ko) A country in North America.

Mija (MEE-hah) Spanish term of endearment meaning "my daughter."

Nacatamales (nah-kah-tah-MAH-les) Traditional Nicaraguan stuffed corn dough.

Nicaragua (nik-ah-RAH-gwah) A country in Central America.

Nueces (noo-WAY-ses) Spanish word meaning “nuts” or “pecans.”

Oaxaca (wah-HAH-kah) A city and state in Mexico.

Ocelot (AHS-eh-lot) A wild cat species native to the Americas.

Pampa(s) (PAHM-pahs) Vast grasslands in South America.

Panama (pa-na-MA) A Central American country.

Pantanal (pan-tah-NAHL) One of the world's largest wetlands.

Papi (PAH-pee) Spanish word meaning “daddy.”

Paraguay (par-ah-GWY) A South American country.

Peru (peh-ROO) A country in South America.

Playa Negra (plah-yah NEH-grah) Black sand surf beach in Costa Rica.

Popocatépetl (poh-poh-kah-TEH-peh-tuhl) An active volcano in central Mexico.

Porcine *(PAWR-sahyn)* relating to or resembling pigs.

Quebracho (keh-BRAH-choh) – A tough South American tree known for its hard wood.

Quechua (KEH-chwa) A Native language family of the Andes.

Saguaro (sah-WAH-roh) A large species of desert cactus.

Señor (sen-YOHR) Spanish word meaning "mister" or "sir."

Shat sirun es (shot see-ROON es) Armenian phrase meaning "you are beautiful."

Somotos Canyon (soh-MOH-tohs KAN-yun) A canyon in Nicaragua.

South America (south uh-MAIR-i-ka) Where most of Juanito's journey takes place.

Spain (SPAYN) A European country where the story begins.

Tango (TANG-go) A style of music and dance from Argentina.

Tangueras (tan-GAIR-as) Female tango dancers.

Tapir (tey-per) A South American mammal resembling an elephant and a pig.

Tarot Card (TAR-ot) Picture cards used for fortune-telling.

Teak (TEEK) A tropical hardwood tree.

Texas (TEK-sus) A state in the southern United States.

Toros bravos (TOR-os BRAH-vos) Fighting bulls bred in Spain.

¡Vamos! (VAH-mos) Spanish word meaning "let's go."

Vaqueros (vah-CARE-os) Cowboys from Mexico or Spain.

Vicuña (vee-KOON-yah) A wild South American animal related to llamas.

Yerevan (yeh-reh-VAHN) The capital and largest city of Armenia

Yucatan Peninsula (yoo-kah-TAN pen-in-SOO-lah): A region in southeastern Mexico.

ընկեր (uhn-KEHR) Friend, companion in Armenian script.

About the author

J.F. McCarney, an award-winning screenwriter and now a novelist, has been a standout in the storytelling realm. His screenplays have earned accolades in the Nicholls Fellowship by the Academy of Motion Pictures Arts and Sciences and the Austin Film Festival. His short film, 'Seeds of Change', released in 2025. He also wrote the popular historical novel, ‘Laika… A Love Story’ inspired by the ill-fated space dog and those that loved her. Fans can also enjoy 'American Vignettes', his series of short audio stories on Spotify and iTunes, showcasing his diverse storytelling talent.

Made in the USA
Middletown, DE
28 April 2025

74835452R00151